SA'LOK

CONQUERED WORLD: BOOK EIGHTEEN

ELIN WYN

CLOCK
WALK
PUBLISHING

TEISHA

"Pull it toward you," I said, raising my voice so that I could be heard over the growl of the hovercraft's twin engines.

Sitting between my legs, Lyrie shifted her weight nervously and reached toward the yoke with her tiny hands.

I laid my hands on top of hers and, being as gentle as I could, I pulled the yoke toward us. The hovercraft's nose pointed up almost immediately, and the engines pushed us away from the ground and toward the bright blue skies overhead.

"Higher, higher," Lyle squealed from behind me, and I let a smile spread across my lips as I obliged.

Tilting the yoke toward me, I used my free hand to

flick a couple of switches on the panel and redirected some extra power to the engines.

Their growl turned into a furious roar, the hovercraft's fuselage rattling and shaking, but neither of the kids showed any fear. If anything, it was the opposite.

The twins were just seven, but they were already as passionate about flying as I was.

Syra, their mother, wasn't exactly happy about it— no mother really enjoys having their children too far away, especially if too far away means being in a metal box hundreds of feet up in the air—but she trusted me with the kids, all the same.

And she was right to do so.

As their aunt, I would never do anything that would really put them in harm's way. I loved them more than I did myself.

But that was life on Ankau.

Risk and reward. They'd have to learn a little bit of the danger soon enough.

"It's all you now," I said as I pushed on the yoke and stabilized the hovercraft. Slowly, I removed my hands from Lyrie's and let her have the controls.

She nodded quietly, an expression of absolute focus washing over her face, and she held the yoke tightly as the hovercraft zoomed through the vastness of the blue sky.

"Bring us back around," I continued. "Tilt it a bit left."

Doing as she was told, Lyrie banked the ship left and settled in a circular trajectory over the woods. Once she straightened the ship, I looked back over my shoulder to ensure Lyle was enjoying himself.

I didn't need to worry.

He had both his hands on the cockpit window, forehead pressed tight against it, and he was looking at the sights with pure fascination.

"Say hi to your mother," I laughed, pointing down at the small outpost right underneath us.

A tall wooden palisade encircled a group of squat buildings, one main road cutting through the outpost from one end to the other. It couldn't even be called a village, but it was home, all the same.

"Where?"

"There," I replied, pointing at the tiny figure standing in front of one of the houses.

It was hard to make out who that figure was from a distance, but I had absolutely no doubt it was Syra. Judging by the time, she was probably hanging the laundry to dry on the clothesline I had set up outside our house.

"Hi, mommy," the twins cried out at the same time, and I had to grab the yoke as Lyrie let go of it to wave at her mother.

Smiling, I reached for the panel and turned one of the engines off, allowing the air resistance to slow the hovercraft down.

Giving a quick glance at all the numbers and metrics on the dashboard—I've always relied more on instinct than on my technical expertise—I started to make a controlled descent, the belly of the hovercraft almost grazing the outpost's wooden palisade as I made a beeline toward our house.

"Already?" Lyle asked, his words thick with disappointment.

"Yeah," I laughed. "You have to do your homework, remember? Your mother will kill me if I keep you away from the books for too long. We'll fly some more tomorrow, alright?"

Carefully, I lowered the hovercraft onto the extension of overgrown grass that separated the house from the shed where I kept the hovercraft whenever I was away.

The clothes hanging outside swayed aggressively as I landed but, thankfully, they held onto the line.

I really, really didn't want to have to redo the washing, and that'd be my fate if the gusts from the hovercraft knocked them down.

"Off you go, kids."

"Homework! Right now," Syra cried out from the

doorway, as if to punctuate what I had just said. She wore an apron over a pair of blue jeans and a faded black t-shirt, but her youthful appearance was betrayed by the stern look on her face.

Her eyes shone in the same way our mother's eyes had whenever she wanted to make it clear we were to obey immediately.

I couldn't help but smile at the memory, despite the twinge of sadness.

The twins jumped out from the hovercraft once I opened the doors, and they marched dutifully inside the house, barely sparing their mother a glance as they went.

I was checking the hovercraft's panel when I noticed Syra was walking toward me.

Placing both her hands on the ship's nose, she gave me a thin-lipped smile, her brown eyes shooting daggers at me through a few locks of her blonde hair.

"I thought we had talked about it," she finally said with a sigh.

"Talked about what?"

"The kids," she replied. "Homework before playing. You know."

"C'mon," I laughed, poking my head out the window just so I could look at her. "Remember when we were kids? Did we ever follow any rule like that?"

"Yeah, well, just wait until you're a mother. That devil-may-care attitude will bite you in the ass."

"Look at you, acting like such a grownup," I teased her.

Popping the pilot's door open, I climbed down from the hovercraft and made my way toward her.

She was still looking at me with a stern expression, but she mellowed out once I kissed her forehead.

Even though she was two years younger than me, Syra had always been the responsible one, and she hated whenever I treated her as if she was the older of the two of us.

It didn't help that I looked younger than I really was.

"I'm serious, Teisha," she sighed. "Life's tough as it is. I just want them to have a shot at a good life."

"I know you do." Laying one hand on her shoulder, I gave it a gentle squeeze and smiled. "And they'll turn out just fine. Those two are some of the brightest kids I've ever come across. And they're brave, too."

"Thank you," she merely said, and this time it was her turn to kiss my forehead. Without saying another word more, she turned on her heels and walked back inside the house.

I stood there, leaning against the hovercraft, and watched her go as the sun started its descent past the horizon line, a bright shade of orange spilling across the sky.

Syra was right—after the war, life had become tough. She had lost her husband during the fight against the Xathi, and was left to raise the two children by herself.

Always keeping her chin up, she fought tooth and nail for the twins to have a happy life.

Even though I didn't worry as much as she did, I could see where she was coming from. I just hoped I was helping more than I stressed her out.

After her husband died, I moved in with her so I could help, but I wasn't really sure about how successful I had been.

There were times when I wasn't around much, always flying on behalf of the Allied League and General Rouhr, and that meant the burden of raising the twins fell on her shoulders alone.

Sure, the money helped, but it only went so far. I was part of a human pilot auxiliary program, and that meant I was on auxiliary wages.

Sometimes I couldn't help but wonder if it wouldn't be better for me to be around the house more often.

I had a degree in linguistics and anthropology—an interest that had taken a back seat once I got my first taste of the open skies—but even if the pay would have been higher, there weren't a lot of university jobs open right now.

Maybe in a few years we'd all be back on our feet,

and I could get something that brought in more money, while allowing me to be home every night to help Syra with the kids.

Someday.

"Come in, Teisha," a voice crackled through my comm unit, derailing my train of thought. *"Are you there?"*

Recognizing the voice as belonging to my favorite K'ver, I smiled as I picked up the small communication device I had hanging from my belt.

"I'm here," I said. "What's up, Sa'lok?"

"Are you free?"

That was Sa'lok.

He never tiptoed around a subject, and he always cut straight to the chase. Most of the aliens were like that, especially the K'ver, but Sa'lok's background as an engineer really defined him as a straight shooter.

A man that was always looking for solutions instead of dwelling on problems.

I liked that.

"Yeah, I'm free," I replied, immediately forgetting all about my plans of having an office job in the city. "Do you need a pilot?"

"I do. I need someone to fly me to Glymna."

"What's there?" I asked him. Glymna wasn't exactly a hub of activity for the general's men, at least the last time I checked.

A small city carved into the earth; it was more like a relic of the first colonists' attempts at urbanization than a proper modern city.

"Don't tell me you're going on vacation," I teased. "There are much better places to visit, you know?"

"*And how would you know that?*" he threw right back at me, his tone one of amusement. "*I don't remember you ever taking a day off.*"

Then, before I could say something, he continued, more serious now. "*There's been a development involving the Gorgos, and I've been asked to consult. The Puppet Master is helping, as well, and Glymna's one of the easiest points of access for him.*"

"Sounds good to me. Where are you?"

"*Nyheim,*" he replied. "*Can you pick me up in an hour?*"

Smiling, I looked at my hovercraft.

It wasn't exactly a pretty model—its maker had filed for bankruptcy even before the war, and its outdated lines were too angular and stern—but I knew every single component hiding under the fuselage.

I had restored and retooled the entire thing myself, after all.

"An hour?" I laughed. "Please, I'll be there in thirty minutes."

"*Won't you need to pack a bag?*"

"Nope." I always kept a go-bag in the cargo hold, one

with everything I needed for at least a week, and that meant I was always ready to go in a minute's notice.

Unlike those pilots that liked taking their time with preparations, I preferred to be ready all the time.

"Then see you soon, Teisha."

SA'LOK

"Stand clear!"

Folding my arms over my chest, I did as I was told and took a couple of steps back as the flight marshal, a spindly human guy in an orange vest, waved his two light sticks and directed Teisha's hovercraft toward the landing pad.

Even though the bright hangar lights bounced off her windshield, I could still see her leaning over the ship's controls, her petite figure and honey-blonde hair enough to make me smile.

"You're late," I told her the moment she climbed down from the hovercraft, her hair cascading down her shoulders in soft waves.

Quickly, she closed the distance between us and punched my arm playfully.

"The kids didn't want me to come," she shot back as an explanation. "But I'm not late. It took me twenty-five minutes to get here. You're the one who arrived early. Seems like someone missed me, huh?"

"Why would I be missing you?" I laughed, cocking one eyebrow up as I grinned. "If I wanted to have someone around to bust my balls all the time, I would have already told the general I want to work with Vrehx."

She pursed her lips and gave me an annoyed look, one that just made me laugh even more. "Come here, you," I told her as I took one step forward and wrapped my arms around her. She happily did the same, resting her head against my chest. "How are the kids?"

"They're growing up fast," she whispered. Against my K'ver frame, she seemed even smaller in comparison, fragile, even. "You should come meet them."

"I'll see if I can ask for a day off once I'm done with Glymna. Your sister, how is she doing?"

"She's fine," she replied, but I could tell by her tone of voice that she wasn't telling me the whole truth.

Not that I was surprised. Syra was still mourning her husband while raising the twins. Never an easy situation to be in.

"Now, what's up with this Glymna business?"

"You heard about the new site one of our archeologists uncovered?"

"I heard a thing or two," she admitted with a small shrug. "But I don't know much about it."

"And you've heard about the new possessions, haven't you?"

"The Gorgoxians, right? Everyone's talking about them."

"Yes, the Gorgos," I nodded, using the shorthand name the teams had been using for the possessed, or the non-corporeal entities who had possessed the poor human hosts. Once the infection had taken place, there really didn't seem to be much difference.

"Apparently some of them were trying to dig a hole right in the middle of the Sika Jungle. It turns out, there was an underground structure there, some sort of holding structure built by an ancient race called the Aeryx. They used it to house those who had been infected by the Gorgoxians."

"So, a prison?"

"Not exactly," I continued. "More like a hospital. I know the general called for a big meeting a couple of days ago, and they figured out that the Aeryx had discovered a way to get rid of the Gorgos. A cure, if you will. Thing is, everything we've managed to get from the structure is in a language we don't recognize. Our Urai friends say that it can be translated, but—"

"You need linguists."

"That's right."

"So, did you call me here as a pilot or as a linguist?"

"Well, I do need to get to Glymna," I smiled. "But you're proficient with languages, and that might come in handy. We'll see how things go. A lab has been set up in Glymna, the best site for the job and the Puppet Master, and we'll be working out of there on a solution."

"Alright, this is an interesting job, I'll give you that much," she said, returning my smile as she tucked a lock of her hair behind one ear.

"But why are you consulting with the guys there? You're not exactly an expert on ancient civilizations or dead languages. Why do they need a chemical engineer, and one that's an expert in biological weapons, to boot?"

Rek. I'd been dreading that question, but I hadn't been able to get through to the general's office yet.

I should have started the process before contacting her. No one should ever fly that fast, especially not a fragile human.

"I can't answer that right now."

I knew that my answer would infuriate her—more than anyone I knew, Teisha hated unanswered questions—but this time I wasn't teasing her or fooling around.

What I had to do in Glymna was classified, general's orders.

I was pretty sure I'd be able to get Teisha the needed clearance, but I still needed the general's authorization for it, and for that, I needed my request to get through. "You're going to have to wait."

Her eyes narrowed, then she shrugged.

"In that case, let's get going."

She might be annoyed, but she'd deal with it. Teisha knew how the military worked as well as any soldier.

Grabbing my bag from the ground, she pressed it against my chest and quickly spun around. I watched her climb into the hovercraft, her movements liquid and smooth, and found myself shaking my head.

Why was she always in such a hurry?

"C'mon, what are you waiting for? You keep standing around like that, and we're gonna die of old age before reaching Glymna."

Once inside Teisha's ship, I waited until the doors were closed to fasten my seatbelt, then fired up my own panel and helped her check if we were ready for takeoff.

Five minutes later, we were leaving Nyheim behind, the brightly lit streets of the city like a sprawling cobweb underneath us. Ahead of us there was nothing but darkness and the clear sky, thousands of shining stars strewn across the nightly canvas.

Sitting behind Teisha, and fully knowing that she couldn't see what I was doing on my screen, I quickly fired off a message to the general and asked for Teisha to be granted the necessary clearance for a prolonged stay in Glymna.

The approval came through ten minutes later.

I hadn't doubted it would, not for a moment.

One of the toughest pilots in the auxiliary pilot program, she had been handpicked by the general as one of the pilots working directly under his orders.

To become one of the general's fliers was an honor few humans had received, and she was the first human woman to get it.

Smart, brave, and talented, she had been an asset for the government ever since the Xathi decided to wreak havoc.

Even more than that, she was also the best company someone like me could have. No matter how dire the situation was, Teisha always kept her head up, and she always had a witty remark on the tip of her tongue.

Whenever she was around, my job became more...fun.

Our friendship was an unlikely one, what with all the anti-alien sentiment going around, but it also felt like the most natural thing to happen.

"You're quiet back there," she called over her shoulder. "You know how nervous that makes me."

"Just considering if I can integrate with your craft from here," I teased. "I'm not sure if my implants can handle something this antiquated."

"Jerk. My baby is a thing of beauty."

I couldn't see her face, but I'd bet a week's pay she'd stuck her tongue out.

Together, we just clicked. Of course, all that just meant I was being constantly harassed by the rest of the guys on my team.

Much like the humans, they had a hard time believing two persons from different genders could become such close friends without anything *interesting* happening.

I didn't pay them much heed.

She was an attractive young woman, no doubt about that, but as much as I liked having her around, I was always so busy that I just didn't have the time to wonder about those things.

Much.

"Up ahead," Teisha finally spoke up after a couple of hours. From behind, looking over her shoulder, I saw bright lights coming straight up from the ground a couple of miles ahead.

"They're signaling us." Without waiting for me to say something, she lowered the power on the engines and dove straight toward the lights.

Only when we were closer did I manage to get a good look at the city.

Unlike most of the cities on the planet, Glymna seemed to grow down instead of up. The place was similar to a gigantic meteor's crater, with the city occupying its inside.

The various districts were like water drops slowly dripping down the inside curvature of a glass.

It was hard not to marvel at the way the monstrous rocky slopes were covered with buildings and streets that had been carved straight into the rock.

Cramped stairs zigzagged through the residential districts, their inclination something that would give pause to those afraid of heights, and there were large openings here and there that seemed to lead into underground tunnels.

No wonder the Puppet Master had wanted us to set up shop here.

"Take us to Hangar C," I told Teisha as I checked my notes. "It's the closest one to the lab, and they're already waiting for us there."

She took us there fast, diving straight into the crater and making the way toward the large metallic structure that jutted out from the rock right near the end of the slope.

"What do I do now?" she asked me as we landed, turning in her seat so that she could look at me. "Wait for you here? Or should I go looking for a hotel to stay in?"

"You're not going to be waiting here," I laughed, already grabbing my bag and opening the hovercraft's door.

Climbing down from the ship, I held one hand out to Teisha. "You're coming with me to the lab."

"I thought you said whatever you're working on was classified."

"It is," I smiled. "But the general gave you clearance on the way over. I was waiting for it, but you swung by too early."

"Does that mean—"

"Yes," I said. "You'll be working with me on this."

"Now you're talking." Jumping out from the cockpit with renewed energy, she offered me a wide grin and then followed me off the landing platform.

A government aide was already on hand to help us, and we followed him out of the hangar and into a maze of underground corridors that led to a sealed vault door.

"Your biometrics have already been inserted into the system," the aide said in a bureaucratic tone, pointing at the panel mounted to the side of the door.

Nodding, I went toward the panel and let it scan my fingerprint and retina.

Immediately, the door hissed as the hydraulics

system came alive and forced it to swing back on its reinforced hinges.

Stepping through the doorway, I glanced back to ensure Teisha was following me, then waited as the door closed again, leaving the aide behind. Ahead of us was an expansive corridor, the walls made of floor-to-ceiling glass panels that offered us a 360-degree view of the various lab rooms.

To our side was the room where a translation team was working on translating the Aeryx languages, and a couple of steps ahead was what seemed like a chemist's lab, all of it packed with state-of-the-art tech.

"This is impressive," Teisha whispered, looking around with a kid's sense of wonder and fascination.

"This is the nerve center when it comes to the Gorgos," I explained. "The general and other staff are the ones pulling the strings, but when it comes to the real action, it's all happening here. Have you met Mariella?"

"Nope," she answered as we stopped next to a human woman who was poring over some text on a computer. She turned to face us and smiled.

"It's amazing what you were able to do with decrypting alien languages," Teisha said. "I've read about some of your work on the 'net. I'm excited to be working with you!"

"Thank you," Mariella said. "I left my notes open on

this network to share with you. But I'm actually off to see the general about another problem." She laughed, swept her hair back into a quick braid. "It's never just one thing at a time anymore, is it?"

We bid her farewell as she hurried away.

"Alright," Teisha nodded quietly, skimming over the files and transferring them to a tablet for reference. "Where are we?"

"The Urai have managed to translate some of the runes we found at the dig site," I explained, turning toward the translation laboratory to watch as the various translators—humans and Urai—worked around a massive table, with a large old-fashioned blackboard mounted against one of the walls.

On it, all manner of runes and possible translations had been drawn up in chalk. "We're in the early stages of the process, but we believe that whatever the Aeryx used had to do with memory."

"Memory? What does that mean?"

"To be honest, I'm not sure," I shrugged. "All I know is that I've been asked to start working on an antidote for the Gorgos' infestation. I plan to start with the chemical processes that relate to memory in humans, and then go from there."

"That's like looking for a needle in a haystack."

"Why would you be looking for a needle there?" I asked her, right before I realized that it had to be one of those human sayings. "Anyway, you're right, it's not an easy task. But with the Puppet Master's help, maybe we'll get somewhere."

"Well, at least we have a plan," she muttered under her breath. Then, turning around, she looked straight at me. "Now, how bad is the infestation? I've been hearing a lot of rumors, but no one really seems to know what's happening."

"Honestly?" Pursing my lips, I hesitated before replying.

In the end, though, I gave it to her straight. More than anyone in my life, she deserved to know the truth.

But still, my stomach knotted.

"It's bad, Teisha. Really bad."

TEISHA

I was thrilled when Sa'lok asked me to stick around. I'd never gotten the chance to be this involved in a mission.

That's why I'd gotten involved as an auxiliary flier in the first place. Of course, the auxiliaries don't actually do anything exciting.

I've been mostly dropping off food and supply packages to remote outposts.

It was rewarding work, to be sure, but ferrying Sa'lok back and forth was my main thrill in life.

I was aware of how sad that was.

Now I had a chance to do something real, something even more meaningful than being a glorified delivery woman.

And I didn't mind getting to spend some extra time with Sa'lok, either.

When Sa'lok handed me a datapad filled with carefully translated notes, I was ecstatic.

"Is this as good as delivering supplies?" Sa'lok asked.

"So much better." I was too excited to even joke with him right now. "You've basically given me the key to a toy shop on Solstice."

"Is that a good thing?" Sa'lok asked.

"A very good thing."

If he wanted to talk further about human metaphors, we'd have to find time later.

Right now, all I wanted to focus on was getting caught up in this wonderful puzzle so I could join the others in the next room.

I found a comfortable corner of the lab, which wasn't an easy feat, as laboratories are notoriously uncomfortable places to lounge.

I flipped through the datapad, glancing at all the materials I could read over.

"How many times has this been translated from one language to another?" I asked Sa'lok. "If I had to guess, I'd say three."

"You'd guess right," Sa'lok replied. "It's a language the team found not long ago. Remember I was telling you about the incident at the dig site?"

"But you didn't finish," I replied, "which is a shame. Descriptive narrative is a strong point of yours."

"Thank you kindly," Sa'lok smirked. "When I was a kid, I liked the idea of becoming a wandering storyteller."

"What stopped you?"

"Realizing that wandering is expensive and storytelling pays nothing," he grinned.

"Yeah, that'll do it," I chuckled. Funny guy, for an engineer. "So, what happened out there?"

"A lot. But what's important right now is that the first language was found on the walls there. The Urai translated the runes, though it's really more of an approximation than an exact translation, and then General Rouhr had them translated into something you humans can read."

"I'll have you know I'm getting really good at reading K'ver."

"Is that so? Pronounce three words in it then," he challenged with a wiggle of his brow.

"I said read, not speak."

Truth be told, I hadn't a clue how his language worked phonetically, and he knew it. I suspect he just wanted an excuse to tease me about it.

"Worth a shot," he shrugged, confirming my suspicions.

"Yes, you're very funny. Now leave me alone to read," I waved him off.

It took only minutes to fall into my old habits. I deeply loved languages and learning about how they fit into different cultures. I truly loved working in the linguistic field. I hadn't realized how much I'd missed it.

I wouldn't give up my current job, though.

On the whole, it's much more practical. It was what the planet needed. More so than linguists, anyhow.

Except for maybe now.

"I see what you mean about memories being an important theme," I said after a few moments. Or, at least, I believed it to be a few moments. One glance at the timepiece told me I'd been reading for the better part of an hour.

"General Rouhr is convinced memories are a solution," Sa'lok said. "So am I."

"Do you really think it's possible?" I set the datapad aside and leaned forward in my chair. "To make chemical memories, I mean."

"Honestly?" Sa'lok gave me a strange look. "There are other things I'd sooner believe."

"That's not very optimistic of you," I frowned.

"Optimists don't make scientific breakthroughs," Sa'lok said. "Realists do."

"Oh please," I rolled my eyes and tried not to laugh.

"You didn't know what an optimist or a realist was a year ago."

"Not true," Sa'lok protested. "I didn't know the human words, but I was familiar with the concepts. My people have our own words for those, not that you'd be able to say either of them."

His smirk made my blood boil, but it also wanted to make me burst out laughing. Sa'lok had that effect on me.

"How long have you two been married?" a passing lab tech asked.

I nearly choked on my breath, heat flooding my checks.

Sa'lok fumbled with the datapad in his hand.

"We aren't married," I said at the same time he said, "We're not together."

"Really?" the tech blinked, "could've fooled me."

"We're friends," I said, even though that must be obvious to the tech.

"Focus on your work," the head scientist of the Glymna lab ordered, looking up. The tech nodded and quickly scuttled out of the room.

"Nothing on that datapad suggests how to make memories, does it?" Sa'lok asked me, turning the topic back to what was important, but with an odd catch in his throat.

"Not that I've seen so far," I replied, pulling my

attention back from wondering what being married to Sa'lok might be like. "I might be able to clarify some of the text, but I won't be able to tell you any new information yet."

"Get clarifying," Sa'lok smirked.

Right. It would be annoying.

But only sometimes...

"Perhaps I might be of assistance?" A calm, layered voice took me by surprise, interrupting my thoughts from going places they shouldn't go.

"When did you get here?" Sa'lok asked, good humor bleeding through his voice.

His gaze was directed at what was, essentially, a standard plant pot. Blooming from it was a rich green plant that looked like a tangle of vines.

"Is that the Puppet Master?" I gasped.

"Indeed," the voice came again.

From the plant.

"How's he talking like that?" I pointed at the pot like an idiot. "Didn't you say the Puppet Master talks into people's minds?'

"He frequently does," Sa'lok replied. "However, it was easier on him for us to figure out a way to project his voice. We used tech similar to the speech pad we made for Fen, the Urai. Look at his pot."

Now I noticed the pot sitting on some kind of dark surface, different from that of the lab table.

"That's basically a speech pad modified in a way the Puppet Master can use," Sa'lok explained. "The pot has no bottom. It's just meant to keep soil from spilling everywhere."

Behind the table was a tangle of vines that lead into the sandstone wall. A hole had been carved into the wall, I suspected for this very purpose.

"I'm so pleased to meet you!" I gushed as I approached the plant. I reached out my hand as if to shake someone else's, and quickly felt silly.

Before I could snatch my hand back, the Puppet Master reached forward with a vine and wrapped it around the width of my hand.

"Pleased to meet you," he, it, the giant entity said. Him. Going with him.

"How can you help?" Sa'lok asked.

"As you know, I can forge a connection with the minds of other sentient beings," he explained. "Part of that is accessing memories. I can see your entire life in the span of a moment. I do not do it often, as I find it to be a violation of privacy. However, I am willing to make a global exception if it means defeating the Ancient Enemies."

"Thank you," Sa'lok nodded. "We don't have much right now. We're hoping you can help with that."

"How may I assist?"

"We have no Gorgo-infected humans here in

Glymna," Sa'lok continued. "However, there are plenty in Einhiv. If you can, I'd like for you to seek one out. Find a subject, reach into its mind, and restore the happiest, brightest, memory you can. We'll work out the next part once you have that."

"I can do that," the Puppet Master replied. "What is the purpose of the happiest memory, might I ask?"

"It's my theory that happy memories are stronger than sad ones," Sa'lok said. "Though I'm not an authority on human psychology. What do human brains prefer?"

I realized Sa'lok was speaking to me, but the lead scientist answered before I could.

"Surely it's sad memories," he said. "The chemicals that create the sad ones are potent."

"I respectfully disagree," I said. "Dopamine is a hell of a drug."

"I don't think a linguist has much authority in the matter," the scientist said smugly.

Seriously?

"We can figure that out as we go," Sa'lok gave me a warning look. He knew my temper was about to snap all over that condescending asshole. "Let's start with a happy, dopamine-filled memory."

"I can do that. Allow me a moment," the Puppet Master said before going silent.

"No!" the scientist barked.

Sa'lok and I stared at him, confused by the sudden outburst.

That's when I saw it. His eyes looked...wrong.

They were glassy, not like a mirror, but like an incredibly clean window.

Sa'lok had told me of this before. It meant a Gorgo was present inside the human. The head scientist had been taken as a host.

"No, no, no, no, no, no, no," the scientist went on, tugging at his own hair as he chanted.

"No, what?" Sa'lok prompted.

He beckoned for me to come to him, so I did.

He pushed me behind him, keeping himself squarely between me and the mad scientist.

"No!" the scientist screamed, and dashed right toward us.

"I'll keep him busy," Sa'lok said. "You need to run."

"Are you kidding?"

Sa'lok grabbed me by the waist and shifted me away from the charging scientist. He careened into a lab table like he didn't know it was there. Glass beakers and vials shattered on the floor.

"Do I sound like I'm kidding?" Sa'lok snapped.

"I'm not leaving you here to deal with that," I insisted.

The scientist charged again.

While Sa'lok drew it to the opposite side of the

room, I grabbed a shard of glass from the floor. It wasn't big. It certainly wouldn't do any lasting damage, not unless I was really lucky.

I couldn't just stand there. I had to do *something*.

I sure as hell wasn't going to leave Sa'lok to deal with this by himself.

I was in a lab, for fuck's sake.

Labs are insanely dangerous places. There had to be something I could use. I glanced around, looking for something to use as a proper weapon.

I smiled when I found just the thing.

SA'LOK

I pulled out a small stun gun and aimed it at the rabid scientist.

"You've had that the whole time?" Teisha shrieked.

I glanced at her.

She looked like she was reaching for something, but I couldn't look away from the enemy long enough to figure out what it was.

"I was waiting for you to get out of the way," I lied.

Truthfully, this little stunner only had a single shot, and Teisha was a distraction.

It was so hard to keep my focus when every instinct in my body was screaming to protect her. That was part of the reason why I'd tried to get her out of here.

Even though she was on the other side of the room

and the Gorgo-infected scientist was totally fixated on me, I still felt frantic for Teisha.

I had the small stun gun ready, but I couldn't make myself pull the trigger. I could tell Teisha was moving. I could see her from the corner of my eye. I didn't dare take my eyes off the scientist.

Damn it, what the skrell was Teisha doing?

The scientist had no hesitations about looking away from me. Perhaps it didn't understand that the small mechanism in my hand was, in fact, a weapon.

"Teisha!" I shouted in warning.

"I'm on it," she called back.

"What? No, don't get on it! Get out!" I shot back.

It was too late.

The scientist whirled on her, teeth bared like some sort of rabid animal. I took aim once more. This wasn't the ideal shot. The scientist was far too close to Teisha.

Teisha held something in both hands. With a mighty swing, she smacked the scientist over the head. He dropped to the floor like a heavy sack of rocks.

Certain the scientist was knocked out, I looked at Teisha. She stood proudly over her victim, clutching a big microscope in her hands.

"That takes care of that," she beamed.

She put the microscope back in its place and examined it.

"It's a bit scratched up now," she frowned. "Oh, well.

It looks like it was his, so I can't say I feel bad." She gave the unconscious scientist a stern look.

"Are you insane?" I sputtered.

"You tell me," she shrugged. "You know me better than anyone."

"In that case, yes, you're insane." Her words sunk in after a moment. "Wait, you think I know you better than anyone?"

"I think so," she said thoughtfully. "My sister knows me very well, but I keep some things from her. I don't want her to worry."

"I'm honored…I think," I thought about her words a little longer. What that might mean…then brushed it away. "You're still insane."

"I'll take your word for it," she grinned. "What are we going to do about this?" She nudged the scientist with the toe of her shoe.

"I have an idea."

I walked over to the pot where the Puppet Master was planted. The speech pad had been cracked in the scuffle, but hopefully the connection would still hold.

I knocked on the pot the way one might knock on a door.

"Excuse me, Puppet Master," I called.

"How can I assist?" the Puppet Master replied.

"We have a situation."

"If you're referring to the scientist, I know."

"Oh." My brows shot up. "How much did you witness?"

"Everything. My apologies for not being able to assist. These tendrils were chosen more for their flexibility than their strength."

"I see," I nodded. "The good news is, you don't have to sift through the hoards over in Einhiv. We have a test subject ready and waiting." I gestured to the scientist.

"Would you like me to harvest a memory?" the Puppet Master asked.

"If you don't mind."

"Not at all."

The Puppet Master snaked a vine across the floor to the unconscious scientist.

"I don't know if I want to know his memories," Teisha said with a small shudder.

"Why not?" I asked.

"Because I don't want to feel guilty for whacking him over the head if he turns out to be a nice guy."

"You didn't hit *him*, you hit an attacking Gorgo using him as a host," I reminded her.

"Either way, he's still the one who's going to wake up with a headache," she pointed out. "If he wakes up."

"If he dies, it's the Gorgo that killed him, not you."

"A subdural hematoma likely wouldn't help the whole staying alive thing," she said.

"Which wouldn't have happened if the Gorgo didn't

choose to take over the body," I said. "Keep trying if you must, but I'm not going to let you take the blame for this."

"Thanks," she sighed heavily. I squeezed her shoulder.

The Puppet Master retracted his vine.

"I have a memory I believe to be suitable to our needs," he announced.

"What is it?" Teisha asked.

"I thought you didn't want to know," I reminded her.

"What can I say? My curiosity won out in the end," she shrugged.

"That wasn't a very long battle."

I grinned when she rolled her eyes.

"Just tell me," she smiled at the Puppet Master. Even though the Puppet Master didn't have a face, I swear he was giving us a judgmental look.

"I chose his mating ceremony," the Puppet Master said.

"His what, now?" Teisha sputtered, going red in the cheeks.

"The ceremony where he stands on an altar with his mate," the Puppet Master said. "They spoke vows and exchanged affections before their families."

"Oh!" Teisha laughed. "His wedding."

Her smile fell. She looked at the scientist.

"Wedding," she repeated. "He has a wife."

"Don't think about it," I told her. "We might be able to flush the Gorgo out of him." I eyed the limp form. "But you're right. Even with the Gorgo in him, he's still a human. Let's make him more comfortable."

Sedated, restrained and hooked to a small device to monitor his vital signs, we'd done our best for the possessed scientist.

"Right," Teisha nodded as she stood from checking his restraints. "Let's get cracking. What do we need to do?"

"That's the tricky part," I winced. "Somehow, I have to get the stored memory out of the Puppet Master and into a vial."

"Any ideas?" she asked.

"One," I replied. "It's a long shot."

"Tell me," she urged.

I didn't speak right away. Yes, I had an idea, but putting it into words that made sense was another matter entirely.

"Puppet Master?" I said.

"Yes?"

"The memories you're able to harvest, are they complete memories or are they snapshots?" I asked.

"It depends on the mind I take the memories from," the Puppet Master replied. "If the subject has an excellent memory and the event is of great significance, I can pull a complete memory. If the subject has a poor memory, or the event happened in the past, I can only get bits and pieces."

"What's the wedding memory look like?" I asked.

Before I could say anything else, the Puppet Master brought a vine to my forehead.

Suddenly, I stood on a rooftop. I recognized the city of Nyheim, though it didn't look the same as it did now. This memory must be from before the Xathi invasion.

I stared at the human woman across from me as if I was looking at her with my own two eyes. In reality, I was looking through someone else's. The memory played out as if it was really happening to me. I felt faint sensations of joy, excitement, and even a touch of fear.

Just before the woman kissed me, the Puppet Master ended the memory.

"There is more than that," he said. "I simply wanted to give you an idea."

"What did you see?" Teisha asked. "You look a little pale."

"It's odd seeing something as if it's happening to you, when it's not," I explained. "Was I meant to feel emotional?"

"I do not know," the Puppet Master replied.

"Did you?" Teisha prompted.

"I felt shadows of emotions," I said. "I could tell the

original owner of the memory felt happy, but I didn't feel it in full."

"Probably because you didn't know the woman standing across from you," Teisha said. "She's a stranger, so you felt indifferent."

"This lends credence to Alyssa's theory." I tapped my chin and started pacing around the room. "We can't pull a single memory and apply it to everyone."

"So, we need to pull a memory from every single person?" Teisha sighed. "That will take far too long. There must be another way."

"I'm sure there is," I said. "I'd rather focus on making the antidote first. If it's viable, we can turn our attention to streamlining the process. Thoughts?"

"That sounds reasonable to me," Teisha said. "I'll keep reading the Urai notes in case there's something we missed."

"Thank you," I smiled at her. "In the meantime, I believe the memory was strong enough for my implants to track the levels of chemicals excreted in the brain during the moment this memory took place." I tapped the screen of my datapad. "I've been working with our lead chemist, Dr. Leena, for weeks now. Between her brilliance and my implants - and a bit of brilliance of my own, we should be able to crack this. Memories can't be bottled, but chemicals can."

"Yes, but those chemicals correlate to feelings and emotions, not images," Teisha pointed out.

She was right. At best, all I could do was make something that mimicked the feelings brought on by the memory.

Maybe that was enough.

"What if I don't need to recreate the memory, just the feeling of the memory? The human brain might recognize the sensations and call up the memory of its own volition," I suggested.

"If you give him a concentrated dose of the exact chemicals his brain secreted during his wedding, that might be enough for him to fight past the mental grip of the Gorgo," Teisha smiled.

"Exactly."

"That doesn't sound too hard," Teisha shrugged.

"You say that now," I shook my head. "But if it doesn't work, I don't have a backup plan."

"You better hope this works then." She grinned over her shoulder as she settled back into a corner of the lab with her datapad. "I'll let you know if I think of any alternate interpretations."

"Much obliged," I replied.

I turned to the Puppet Master, arms folded across my chest.

"Now, let's see about getting that memory out of you."

TEISHA

When Sa'lok told me he was going to be working with chemical memory processes, I never thought I'd end up connecting electrical sensors to a bunch of vine tendrils.

But there I was, wearing a white coat and hooking up tiny green tendrils to a brain scanner. It was a weird turn of events, but I no longer questioned the weirdness of it all.

After all, I lived in a world where aliens existed, ancient races were possessing human bodies, and plants had become self-aware.

Weird was the new normal.

"I think we're good to go," I muttered as I double-checked my work. I wasn't exactly a specialist when it came to all those biotech procedures, but I was fairly confident I could hook up a bunch of sensors without screwing up.

There were other scientists in the building that could've assisted Sa'lok with this, but none of them were around this late at night.

Instead of waiting till morning, he had decided to start working right away, and enlisted me as his assistant. "Are you sure this is going to work?"

"*Yes,*" a disembodied voice whispered inside my mind, and only then did I notice that a tiny vine had coiled itself around my ankle, its soft surface brushing against my skin. "*I can mimic the way the human brain works. Your machines should be able to read the electric signals coming from me, just as well as they'd read the ones coming from a real human brain.*"

"The Puppet Master's right," Sa'lok added. He was sitting in the corner, hunched over a large holographic screen.

It was an unusual sight; far taller and more muscular than a regular human man, Sa'lok had a scientist's brain trapped inside a warrior's body.

It was far easier to imagine him carrying a high-powered rifle and mowing down a horde of Xathi than it was to see him here, quietly trying to make sense of a mountain of data.

"All we need to do is register the electric signals

attached to the specific memories we want, and then extrapolate the specific chemical levels in the brain."

"How about you try that again, as if you wanted me to follow it."

Swiveling his chair around so that he was facing me, Sa'lok leaned back and draped his arms over the armrests.

"Think of the brain as a gigantic computer made up of neurons and synapses. That's what we use to create and store new information, and we activate those neurons and synapses through a mixture of chemicals and electricity. If we can pinpoint the electric signals that elicit a specific response, we might be able to deduce the chemicals involved in the process."

"I'm going to pretend that I understood it all," I laughed. I was far more comfortable with ancient runes than with brain chemistry, no doubt about it. "You're saying that, if we manage to get a correct readout, you'll be able to create a chemical cocktail that'll be able to elicit that guy's wedding memory on command?"

"That's the plan," he replied, turning back toward his screen and typing something on his keyboard. Without looking at me, he continued. "The Puppet Master will help us create a memory blueprint, and from there...well, I'm not exactly sure what I'll be able to do, but we gotta start somewhere."

"How the hell do you know so much about the

human brain?" I asked him. The *Vengeance* hadn't landed here that long ago, but Sa'lok's knowledge seemed to rival that of the top scientists working in the field. "I mean, I know you're a chemical engineer and all that, but the human brain is something else entirely."

"I was curious about you," he shrugged. "Not you specifically," he quickly added, and I could almost swear there was a note of embarrassment in his voice. "I've been curious about your species ever since I landed here. I didn't have much time to research during the war against the Xathi, but once that was done, I made sure to visit the library in Nyheim and—"

"Oh my God," I muttered, cupping my mouth with one hand while I feigned shock. "You're such a nerd."

"Thank you."

"That wasn't completely a compliment, you know?" I laughed. Even though he seemed to have researched humans extensively, some of our little speech nuances and slang still seemed to elude him.

I actually found that quite charming.

He was better now, though; the first time we met, he'd taken everything I said at face value, no matter how silly it was.

"Alright, we're ready," I announced again, this time completely sure I had hooked the Puppet Master to the scanner correctly.

"Perfect." Jumping up from his seat, he walked across the lab toward the main computer terminal.

I joined him and watched as his fingers flew over the keyboard, quickly turning the machine on and initiating the scanning procedure.

I didn't say a word as a bunch of data started marching across the holographic screen in front of us, myriad data showing up faster than I could process it.

It all seemed like random nonsense to me anyway, but the expression of pure concentration on Sa'lok's face was enough for me to know the procedure was working as intended. Even if, instead of a human brain, we had to work with a plant.

"Not just a plant," the Puppet Master said, and I was startled in place.

The cracked speech pad had finally failed, and I still hadn't gotten used to the way he could read my mind.

I was a transparent kind of girl, and I always spoke my mind, but to have someone know what I was thinking before I could say it out loud was slightly unsettling. *"Don't worry, everyone thinks the same at first."* I smiled at that.

Even though it would take some time before I got used to it, I didn't feel like the Puppet Master was an intruder. His presence felt friendly and reassuring, like warm gloves on a cold winter morning.

"I think I got it," Sa'lok announced after a couple of

minutes of staring at the screen. "As I thought, dopamine holds the key when it comes to positive memories. I'm also going to need oxytocin, serotonin and endorphins."

"What about salt and pepper?"

"What?" he asked, confusion clouding his eyes. Then, as if he suddenly got that I was making a joke, he opened up into a smile. "I see, a joke. Good one. You're actually right—even though I won't need salt and pepper, this is going to be a lot like cooking."

"And are you a good cook? Because I'm a disaster."

"I'll teach you one of these days," he laughed, his eyes locked on mine, and I felt blood warm my cheeks.

As friendly as we were, we mostly just hung around because of work.

We had never spent time together on a personal basis, and to think of that happening...well, I didn't know what to make of it, but I sure liked the thought of it.

Clearing my throat, I looked away from him. "What do you need me to do?"

"Submit this order to the lab administration," he quickly replied, typing up a list of chemicals and their dosages on the keyboard. "See if they have what we need in stock. I want to get started right away."

"Aye, aye, captain," I teased him, but did as I was

told. Ten minutes later, a young lab assistant was wheeling a sealed cart inside the room.

I hung back as Sa'lok worked his magic, pacing back and forth between the various computers and machinery as he tried to mix the right dosage of the chemicals, and did my best to help whenever he asked me to.

I wasn't exactly feeling useful—there were only so many utensils I could pass him—but I didn't mind it; it felt comfortable to be around him.

The night slipped away faster than I was expecting, and it was already early morning when Sa'lok jumped to his feet and grinned wildly. "It's done," he announced, hands on his hips as he looked at the small vial in front of him, a clear liquid resting inside it. "I have no idea if this is going to work, or what effects it'll produce, but I think we're onto something."

"What now?" I asked, looking toward the corner of the lab where the unconscious scientist still lay sedated and restrained.

Even though I didn't like it, the fact that he had been infected by the Gorgo meant that we had to take some precautions. "Can we use it on him?"

"Not while he's unconscious," Sa'lok whispered, a slight frown showing on his face. He only seemed to be considering it now, and his disappointment was almost palpable. "I don't know if he'd receive the memory in a dream or not. It's too many variables to account for."

For a guy that always accused me of being in a hurry, he sure didn't look like he was willing to wait for the poor guy to wake up.

But I hated to see him so disappointed.

"How are you going to administer it, anyway?"

"Just a few drops under the tongue should do it," he replied. "That's the quickest way to get it into his system. I guess we'll have to wait until he's awake, and then we'll try."

Walking past him, I grabbed the small vial as carefully as I could, pinching it between my index finger and thumb, and narrowed my eyes at the sloshing liquid inside. "This looks like water," I said. "Or acid. Are you sure this is safe?"

"Yes. Worst case scenario, it won't do a thing. Maybe provoke some mild euphoria."

"That doesn't sound too bad," I whispered, an idea suddenly bursting into my mind. "Why don't *I* give it a try?"

"What are you saying?" he asked me, disbelief all over his face.

"I'm saying that I want to test it on myself," I announced, looking away from the vial and into Sa'lok's eyes. "You don't want to wait, and I don't want to wait. So let's just get this over with."

SA'LOK

"**A**re you out of your mind?"

"What?" Taking a step back, Teisha raised both eyebrows and clutched the vial against her chest. "You said it's harmless. So what's the harm in trying it on me? The way I see it, there's no downside."

She had me there.

Still, even though I believed that my chemical cocktail was perfectly safe, there were a lot of unforeseen complications that could arise.

By testing it on the Gorgo-infected scientist, I would be taking a controlled risk.

But with Teisha...no, I couldn't risk it, even if there was virtually zero danger to what she wanted to do.

"Please, Teisha, give me the serum," I asked her,

holding my hand out. "As sure as I am, I don't want to take unnecessary risks. You're not infected, and—"

Before I could continue, Teisha popped the cap off the vial with her thumb. A small smile spread across her lips and, as a response, I frowned. "Don't do anything stupid."

"Like what?" she laughed, sticking her tongue out in a playful manner.

By the ancestors! How could she be acting like this? "You didn't lie to me, did you? This thing won't kill me, will it?"

"No, I don't think so, but—"

"And then we can find out if it works for more than one person, right? Progress." Holding the vial up, she brought it to her lips and carefully allowed some of the liquid to touch them.

Once she was sure there were a few drops under her tongue, she placed the cap back on the vial and finally surrendered it to me.

"You're insane."

"Thank you," she smiled.

"That wasn't meant as a compliment."

"I know." Turning around, she placed both hands on her hips and looked down at her body. "What happens now? Am I supposed to be feeling something? Because I feel perfectly normal."

"I'm not sure," I admitted. Never having tried the serum before, I had no idea what its effects would be.

Even though I was worried about Teisha, it was slightly disappointing to see that the serum wasn't doing anything at all.

I was already tweaking the formula in my head when Teisha staggered back.

"Hang on," she muttered, her voice mellowing out. Placing one hand on the desk beside her for support, she closed her eyes and a lazy smile dawned on her lips. "I think I might need a seat," she continued, and I could already see her knees starting to buckle.

Moving fast, I grabbed a chair and placed it behind her. "Much better now," she said as she sank into it.

"What's going on?" I was trying to hide any excitement from my voice, but it was impossible. Something was happening. "Talk to me, Teisha, what are you feeling?"

"Have you ever taken any drugs?" Draping both arms over the armrests, she leaned back and sighed. "I haven't. I guess you haven't either. You're too much of a by-the-rules kind of guy. But if I had to guess, this feels like a drug. It's as if I'm floating."

I didn't know if that was a good thing or not, but I reached for her and laid one hand on her knee to anchor her.

"You feel good, then?"

"Are you kidding? I feel more than just good." Suddenly, she sat straight in the chair, and her eyelids fluttered open. "I feel...oh, God, I feel just like I felt when the twins were born." Looking straight into my eyes, she laid her hand on top of mine, her tiny, delicate fingers wrapping around and squeezing mine, and her voice dropped into a gentle whisper. "I feel happy."

I said nothing at that. I just took in every detail of her perfect face, stray wisps of hair falling over her forehead.

Her cherry lips were slightly parted, and each breath she drew was gentle and smooth. She looked relaxed...and beautiful.

"I can smell it, you know?" she whispered, closing her eyes again. "The scent of their tiny blankets as I held them for the first time. And I can see it, too. Syra, with her disheveled hair and tired smile, lying on the hospital bed. Lyrie and Lyle, too. God, they were so tiny."

"That's a good memory, right?" The answer was an obvious one, but I still needed to hear her say it.

"The best memory," she replied in that sleepy tone. Lazily, she opened her eyes and reached for my face, gently cupping it with the open palm of her hand. "Thank you, Sa'lok."

"What for?"

"For making me remember." Taking a deep, soft

breath, she continued. "It's hard to explain, but the way I'm remembering it...it's all so vivid. It's almost as if I'm back there again." She paused for a moment, then ran the tip of her tongue over her lips. "Can you get me some water? My throat feels dry."

Grabbing some bottled water from the small refrigeration unit in the breakroom, I returned to her side as fast as I could. "Here," I said, pushing the bottle into her hands after unscrewing the cap. "Drink up."

"Thank you," she whispered, her voice regaining some strength. "I feel so goddamn thirsty."

I made a mental note of that, and then held one hand out.

She looked at it for a moment, confused, and then grabbed it.

"I just want to see if you can stand up," I explained as I pulled her up to her feet. As she did, I smiled as I saw her standing straight, with no noticeable swaying or staggering. "Good, it looks like the serum's wearing off."

"Yeah, I can feel it," she nodded. "That was like going from sober to drunk, then sober again, in just a couple of minutes. I just hope this stuff won't leave me nursing a hangover."

"I can't promise you that." Laying one hand on her shoulder, I smiled. "But even if it does, it was worth it."

"It was?" she blinked slowly, still a bit confused.

"Yes. What happened to you means that we don't

need to target specific memories for every single person. There's no need to customize the serum, at least as far as I can tell." My mind flew ahead, making notes to send to the main lab.

"Right now, it seems like the formula is enough to trigger general feelings of happiness, love, and excitement...and those feelings are what will circle someone's mind to the happiest memories they have. I thought I'd have to tweak the formula for each person, as every person has different triggers, but it seems like the serum has a blanket effect. That's the theory, anyway."

"You did it," Teisha cried out, "you really did!"

"Hold on, we don't know that for—"

Before I had the chance to finish my sentence, she closed the distance between us and wrapped her arms around my torso.

My heart kicked and punched against my ribcage as I felt her delicate body pressed against mine and, reacting on instinct alone, I cradled her head with one hand as I held her close.

We lingered in each other's arms for a long moment, then Teisha pulled slightly back and looked into my eyes.

"We make a great team, don't we?" she asked me, her words soft.

"Yes, we do," I found myself saying, my voice

nothing but a whisper. Slowly, my eyes were drawn to her parted lips.

For a moment, I wondered how they'd taste, how it'd feel to pull her in and simply go for it.

With one hand resting on the nape of her neck, I kept my eyes on hers and leaned in, my instincts somehow bypassing my rational mind.

Our lips were mere inches apart when a loud crash broke the moment.

"What the hell?" Teisha cried out, turning around fast.

I did the same, just in time to see a vine slithering away from the spot on the floor where the vial with the serum lay shattered.

"You broke it?" I shook my head, confused, instinctively reaching for one of the vines that snaked up a pipe that ran across the wall. "Puppet Master, why would you do that?"

I expected to feel the warmth of the Puppet Master's presence, but it simply wasn't there.

There was a kind of brittle coldness in its place, one that I didn't exactly care for. "Why would you do such a thing?" I insisted, anger getting the best of me.

Wrapping my fingers around the vine in my hand, I did my best not to crush it in anger. When I didn't get an answer, I raised my voice. "Answer me!"

"They're here," came a faint whisper, and all of a

sudden, the vines inside the lab started thrashing around haphazardly.

I felt the vine in my hand squeezing my fingers back, and I saw Teisha grimace as the one wrapped around her ankle started tightening up. *"They're here."*

"Who's here?" I asked, looking around the lab to see it completely deserted.

Aside from Teisha, all the other scientists were still in their quarters, and it'd be an hour or two before they'd start marching back into the lab. "I don't understand."

"They're here," the Puppet Master repeated one last time, and then the vines grew limp.

They fell onto the floor as if dead.

The only thoughts inside my head were my own.

I tried to close my eyes, just to see if I could focus and hear the Puppet Master's voice, but it was useless.

The Puppet Master was gone.

TEISHA

"What the hell just happened? What did the Puppet Master mean by 'they're here'?" My voice sounded more panicky than I expected it to be, but that was to be expected, given the circumstances.

One of our long-standing allies had just gone berserk, and we had no idea why.

"You heard it too?" Sa'lok asked me, his eyes wide with confusion. Hesitantly, he reached for the vine wrapped around his wrist and peeled it off. Its color was still bright green, but it was limp and lifeless otherwise.

The moment Sa'lok opened his hand, the vine just fell to the floor, offering no resistance.

"Yeah, I heard it," I replied, looking around the lab as I wrapped my arms around my body.

The Puppet Master's last words had been ominous ones, and a feeling of dread and anxiety was starting to take over me.

What exactly had he meant? Was someone coming our way?

Had the Gorgos managed to find out about the Glymna lab?

When I told Sa'lok about my fears, he pursed his lips tightly and reached for the comms unit on his belt.

"This is Sa'lok speaking," he started to say, "I'm currently in lab 06. I need a perimeter update. Any breaches or suspicious activity to report?"

"*Nothing at all, sir,*" a voice crackled past the static of the comm. "*Everything's quiet. Nothing to report in the lab perimeter, or even in the city.*" There was a slight pause then, and when Sa'lok didn't say anything, whoever was on the other end of the line decided to continue, although somewhat hesitantly. "*Do we have any reasons for concern?*"

"No, not right now," Sa'lok replied, but I noticed the way his fingers tightened around the comms unit, his knuckles turning white. "Just keep your guard up."

"*Will do, sir.*"

"I'm so confused," I admitted, raking one hand over my face as I said it. "If there's no one trying to break into the labs, then what the hell was the Puppet Master talking about? And why did he knock over the serum? None of this makes any sense."

Gritting his teeth, Sa'lok pinched the bridge of his nose, a gesture he always did whenever he wanted to focus.

He took a couple of deep breaths, and then exhaled sharply through his nose. "Maybe he wasn't talking about the labs," he finally said. "Maybe he was talking about something else."

"Something else? Like what?" Then, before he could reply, it dawned on me. I knew that the Puppet Master's core—or brain or heart or whatever it was—was hidden under a complex system of underground tunnels out in the desert.

The teams under General Rouhr's command made regular trips there and, as Sa'lok had once told me, even anti-alien militants had attacked it once.

"Someone's there with the Puppet Master." I swallowed hard. "Someone he doesn't like."

"That's the most likely scenario," Sa'lok breathed out through gritted teeth. He clenched and unclenched his fists repeatedly, and I could tell he wasn't sure of what he should do next. "That probably explains why he tried to destroy the serum. It was, after all, the first potentially working cure we had for pushing the Gorgos out of their host bodies."

"I don't get it," I said. "You think the Puppet Master has been infected?"

"I'm not sure. But that would explain a lot, wouldn't it?"

"God, what a mess," I sighed, sinking back down onto the chair.

While earlier I had sat because I was feeling happy and drowsy, now I sat down because I didn't know what else to do.

Sa'lok didn't say a word for about a minute, but when he finally spoke up, there was no indecision in his voice. He had looked at the facts we had from every angle, like a true engineer, and he had reached a decision.

"Come on." Taking my hand, he pulled me up to my feet. I came up so fast that the chair I had been sitting on toppled to the floor. "We're going there."

"To the Puppet Master's lair?" I asked him, even though I already knew what the answer would be. "I've never been there."

"I've been there before a couple of times," he continued as he dragged me out of the lab and into the partially lit corridor. "I'll guide you." We made our way toward the sealed door with quick strides and, once it swung back to let us out, it took all we had not to break into a run.

"Wait." I stopped all of a sudden and, before Sa'lok

could protest, I grabbed his arm and forced him to stop. He spun around, not looking too happy, but he waited for me to continue. "The scientist. We left him back at the lab."

"Rek," he growled, and grabbed his comms unit. "This is Sa'lok speaking."

"*Officer Mitchell here,*" the voice from before replied. "*If you want to know about the perimeter, everything's the same as it—*"

"I need you to pay close attention to what I'm going to say," Sa'lok cut him short. Grabbing my hand, he started walking again, leading the way through the maze of underground corridors. "I want you to call whoever you need to and give the hovercraft I flew in on clearance for a flight out of the city."

"*That's done, sir. Ships transporting government officials are free from—*"

"Then I want you to head into the scientists' quarters and wake up whoever's doing the morning shift in lab 06."

"*They won't be too happy about—*"

"Just do it," Sa'lok growled. "By now they're probably aware that one of them has been infected by the Gorgos. Tell them they'll find him bound inside the lab, and that they're to keep him safe, unharmed, and to monitor him."

"*Alright,*" the officer said. "*May I ask what this is all—*"

Before officer Mitchell could finish his sentence, Sa'lok pressed a button on his comms unit and severed the connection. Placing it back on his belt, he then started walking faster.

I was almost having to run just so I could keep up with him.

"I'm sorry, Teisha." Throwing me a quick glance over his shoulder, he gave me an apologetic smile. "Time is of the essence. If the Puppet Master is in danger, we must act now."

"What about the other teams?"

"We'll call it in on the way," he replied. "But if I remember the last schedule, they're all too far away." His jaw tightened. "We'll get there before any of them do. But I'll inform the general, all the same." Punching the top button on the elevator panel in front of us, he shifted his weight from one foot to the other as we waited for the doors to slide back into their partitions.

Once they did, Sa'lok almost jumped inside.

He leaned against the wall and started fiddling with his comms unit once more. "Get me the general," he growled once he found the frequency he had been looking for.

"Sa'lok?" A voice I didn't recognize said. "What's going on? It's still early, the general is asleep."

"Then wake him up. Right now."

A couple of seconds later, the deep but sleepy voice of the general filled the cramped space of the elevator.

"This better be good, Sa'lok."

"I have reason to believe the Puppet Master is under attack right now," Sa'lok explained, not bothering with any small talk. "It's also possible that he has been infected by the Gorgos."

"Blast," the general exclaimed, his voice tense. I found it strange that he was using an expression that only humans used, but that was probably normal—he had, after all, taken a human as his mate. *"All the teams are deployed right now. I'll try and redirect someone right away, but it might take them a while to get there. I think you might need to head there yourself. Take the best pilot you have with you."*

"She's with me now, sir," Sa'lok responded without a moment's hesitation, and I felt my heart swelling with pride at that. "And we're already on the way."

"Good. Then keep me updated. And I don't think I need to tell you this, but whatever you have to do to keep the Puppet Master safe...do it. More than just being an important asset, he's this planet's beating heart. We can't afford to lose him."

"Understood, sir."

"What if it's too late?" I asked Sa'lok once he put the comms unit away. "What happened in the lab wasn't normal. If the Puppet Master has already been infected, then I don't know what—"

"One thing at a time," Sa'lok cut me short, hushing me by placing one of his fingers over my lips.

Then he smiled. Everything was spiraling out of control and he was actually *smiling*. "That's what you always tell me, right? I'm used to telling people you're a pro at keeping a level head, so don't make me look like a fool, deal?"

"I'll try."

"It'll be alright, Teisha, we just need to get there as fast as we can."

"Then leave it to me." As the elevator doors opened to reveal the spacious hangar, I took a deep breath.

My hovercraft was still on the landing pad, which meant I wouldn't need more than ten seconds to get us out of here.

"Fast is my middle name."

SA'LOK

"Are you sure this is safe?" Clutching the armrests of my seat, I looked out the window as the fuselage covering the twin engines started turning red from the heat.

The trepidation was almost as intense as when you cut through the atmosphere of a planet and every bolt seemed to be rattling in place.

Outside, the scenery was flying past us so fast I had to stop looking out the window.

"Are you afraid?" Teisha laughed, her voice brimming with excitement. Whatever anxiety she had been feeling had now given way to an adrenaline rush.

"I'm not afraid," I protested. "But don't you think you're going a bit too fast? I'd like to get to the Puppet Master in one piece, if possible."

"One very *timely* piece," she added and, flicking some switches on her control panel, directed whatever energy the hovercraft still held in reserve toward the engines.

A whining sound started making itself heard, one that made my eardrums hurt, and I was pushed back against my seat so hard that all the air left my lungs.

We cut through the pre-dawn skies like a bullet, and I actually had to close my eyes to control how nauseous I was feeling.

I had never become nauseous before—at least not when it came to flying—and I was just thankful I hadn't eaten breakfast. If I had, it would probably be lining the floor around my feet already.

"Alright, you can breathe out now," Teisha added, and I felt the ship slowing down. The whining sound stopped, the clattering of metal on metal became almost inaudible, and the world outside my window became more than a simple blur. "We're two minutes away from the tunnel entrance."

"Already?" The trip from Glymna to the Puppet Master's lair should've taken at least two hours, but if Teisha was right, it had taken us less than an hour. "How's that even possible?"

"Why do you think the general wanted me as one of his pilots?" Looking back at me over her shoulder, she patted the control panel and grinned.

"I guess I've found something you didn't know about me." She stroked the panel again, and for a moment I felt a wave of... jealousy? Impossible. "More than being a good pilot, I'm also a good mechanic. I've fitted two dozen state-of-the-art injectors around the engines, and tweaked their cores so that they'd be able to process the extra fuel."

"Impressive."

"Thanks," she smiled, looking proud about her handiwork. She had every right to be—when it came to it, Teisha was probably even more talented than some of the mechanics and pilots we had in our old *Vengeance* crew.

"Look, down there." Pointing toward a wide crater about two hundred feet below us, I gritted my teeth as I saw half a dozen aerial units and hovercrafts idling around its rim. I didn't need a closer look to know that those weren't governmental units.

The general had installed proximity sensors around the crater, but whoever was here had somehow managed to deactivate them.

"Do you recognize any of those ships?" Teisha asked me, already dipping the hovercraft's nose and starting our descent.

"Unfortunately, I do," I replied. "A number of them were reported as stolen in Nyheim over the last few weeks." I stretched out my shoulders. "It seems we were right. Someone's trying to get to the Puppet Master. Land behind that dune over there," I continued, pointing toward a spot that I hoped would conceal our ship. "We don't know if there are more of them coming."

Three minutes later, my boots hit the rocky ground. Grabbing my rifle from the cargo hold, I ensured the batteries were fully loaded and that I had all the ammo I needed.

"You're expecting a fight?"

"It's likely," I admitted, feeling the weight of the rifle in my hands. It had been a while since I'd had the chance to use it, and I wasn't exactly looking forward to it. "According to the last communication I received from HQ, the general has already sent a team our way. They'll be here in an hour and a half."

"We can't wait for them," she said, and for once I agreed with her impatience.

Still, I didn't want to risk Teisha's life, and we were clearly outnumbered. The logical thing for us to do would be wait for backup, but if we simply hung back and waited...

"You're right," I nodded. "We can't afford to lose the Puppet Master. You stay here and I'll go ahead to—"

"Yeah, no," she cut me short, rummaging through the boxes in the cargo hold and grabbing a small handgun from inside one. "If you think I'm gonna sit here while you go into the tunnels, then you're in for a surprise. I'm coming with you."

"Fine," I sighed. There was no use arguing with her. Whenever she set her mind on something, not even the general himself would've been able to stop her. "Just be careful."

"Always am," she smiled, tucking her handgun into her belt.

Removing her lab coat, she threw it into the cargo hold and then locked the doors.

Underneath her coat she had a simple black tank-top, one that immediately drew my attention to the way her breasts strained against the fabric.

Get a grip, I chided myself. We were about to step into a life-risking situation and here I was admiring the shape of her body.

Why was it so hard to focus whenever she was around me? Clearing my throat, I gave myself a little encouraging nod.

"Follow me," I told her as I started going up the dune, my boots sinking into the sand. As we reached the top, I lay flat on my stomach and peeked over the edge.

There was no one else in the crater, which meant whoever was inside the tunnels hadn't bothered with a lookout. Instead of going straight toward the crater, though, I led Teisha away from it.

The intruders probably weren't aware of it, but a hidden set of stairs had been built in an ancillary crater, allowing the general's men to get to the bottom caverns faster.

We made our way down the narrow stairs that had been carved into the slope of the crater, doing it as quietly as we could so we could pay attention to any noises ahead. As the stairs finally sunk underground, cutting a straight path through the maze of tunnels, a deep silence enveloped us.

It seemed I had been right, and that whoever was trying to get to the Puppet Master hadn't known about this access point.

"Is that normal?" Teisha whispered once we got to the bottom caverns, the sound of dripping water the only thing keeping us company.

The flashlight attached to my rifle was lighting the path ahead, but it seemed like the usual way to the Puppet Master's heart had been blocked.

Thick vines, some of them thicker than my forearm, had been woven together into a massive wall.

"No," I replied, carefully reaching for the vines with one hand. I brushed my fingertips against them, hoping to feel that familiar presence, but there was nothing. "He's trying to keep us out."

"Maybe it's to protect us."

"Maybe."

Pointing the flashlight at the vine blockade in front of us, I tried to find a weak point in the structure.

Noticing the way the two thickest vines were interwoven, I handed Teisha the rifle, then grabbed one of them with both hands.

I placed one foot against the wall for leverage and, holding my breath, started pushing the vine back with as much strength as I could muster.

It wasn't easy, and my muscles readily started complaining from the effort, but I eventually managed to create a small opening we could use to squeeze through.

I wanted to go first and check the path ahead, but Teisha handed me the rifle and immediately went through the gap in the vines.

"Path's clear," she said, and then grabbed my hand and helped me through. I was far larger than she was, and I struggled not to get stuck.

Eventually, though, I got to the other side.

"We're close now," I whispered, careful to keep my voice low. If the Puppet Master had put up a barrier to keep us out, then that probably meant whoever had stolen the aerial units were already down here as well.

I slung my rifle over one shoulder, letting my vision shift over to add more infrared to account for the darkness.

Leading Teisha, we started making our way through

the tunnel, but we had only gone a few yards when I heard the shuffling of heavy boots up ahead.

"Skrell," I muttered, immediately pointing my rifle toward the sound.

A faint yellow light came from a few feet ahead of us, right where the tunnel bent left, and I could see human shadows being cast against the wall.

"Who's there?" I heard a man's voice asking, and I immediately dropped to one knee, waiting for someone to step into my line of fire.

Teisha followed my lead, crouching next to me while holding her handgun with both hands. "Come out right now!"

I said nothing.

I just held my breath and waited.

When the first man stepped into sight, I pointed toward his leg and fired, the sound of it echoing like thunder through the tunnel. Hurt and disoriented, he crashed against the wall with a deep groan, then doubled over and collapsed on the ground.

Behind him came six more men, but they were wiser than the one leading them. Instead of charging ahead, one of them grabbed a grenade from his belt pouch and rolled it toward us.

Knowing there was no chance we'd be able to get past the vines before the grenade exploded, I reacted on instinct and threw myself on top of Teisha, covering her small body with mine.

This is it, I thought, *the end of the line for me.* Except, it wasn't. Instead of exploding, the grenade went off with a loud pop and filled the entire tunnel with clouds of smoke.

"Zet," I growled, taking aim once more. "I should've known."

It was too late. The six men were already on us, the muzzles of their rifles pointing straight toward us. I reacted fast and, grabbing one of the muzzles, rammed the butt of the rifle against its owner's chest.

At the same time, I spun around and kicked one in the groin while elbowing another, the nauseating sound of a nose being broken echoing throughout the tunnel.

"Put that mechanical bastard down," one of them cried out, and someone yanked the rifle out of my hands.

Two of them directed their attention toward Teisha, punching her in the stomach and knocking her down, while the rest of them descended upon me like a pack of aramirion.

They punched and kicked like men possessed, and I only stopped offering any kind of resistance when one of the bastards pointed his rifle at Teisha.

"Alright, you alien sicko," he spat, his yellowed teeth showing in his tired grin. "You're coming with us right now, or I'm going to put a bullet in your girlfriend's head."

"I'll kill you," I growled, a cocktail of anger and adrenaline coursing through me. Still, I did as I was told and lowered my arms.

As one of the men started binding my wrists, I couldn't resist issuing them one final warning.

"You touch one hair on her head and I'll kill the lot of you. That's a promise."

TEISHA

"Walk," one of the men said, prodding me with his blaster. A lanky guy with an overgrown stubble, he had dead eyes that didn't seem to care much about the world around him. He kept one hand on my shoulder to guide me, the other keeping the muzzle of his weapon pressed against my lower back.

"I'm walking," I threw right back at him, doing my best not to stumble as we advanced through the dimly-lit tunnels.

My wrists had been bound with rope, and it had been tightened so much that I could feel the restricted blood pounding.

Sa'lok walked a couple of feet ahead of me, but instead of having one man guiding him, he had four of them. No one was taking any risks around him, it seemed, especially after he had shot one in the leg and broken another's nose.

"Faster," the man behind me said, poking my lower back once more.

"I'm going as fast as I can." Looking back at him over my shoulder, I gave him my death-stare. "Just who the hell are you, anyway, and what are you doing here?"

"Mind your own business, you alien-loving bitch," he snapped, clearly enjoying the fact that he was in control. Even though he didn't strike me as the smartest one in the whole bunch, it seemed like he was actually capable of some conversation.

The fact that whatever they were doing here had required some careful planning seemed to discredit the theory that these men were working under the Gorgos' influence. They were assholes, but they weren't rabid, infected assholes.

It took us a couple more minutes before we stepped into a large underground chamber, the Puppet Master's beating heart right at the center. It looked like a large plant's bulb, bigger than a regular human being, and it seemed like it was breathing...or beating, just like a heart.

Around it were at least two dozen humans—most of them were men, but there were a few women as well—and all of them were armed. They had a scraggly appearance, with most of the men having ragged beards, but they all looked alert.

"Anyone else roaming the tunnels?" a woman asked, stepping forward to face our captors. As for Sa'lok and me, she barely spared us a glance, although I noticed her upper lip trembling with disgust as her gaze flew over Sa'lok.

These assholes were part of an anti-alien faction, that much was clear.

"There's no one else," the man that had been guiding me replied. "Just these two."

"Good," the woman said, her tone even and controlled. Walking toward me, she offered me a thin-lipped smile. "The name's Amenya. I'm sorry we had to bind you, but your *pet* here didn't leave us much choice."

"He's not my pet." I didn't bother with returning her smile. I just glared at the bitch, wishing for her to take one step closer just so I could headbutt her. She wasn't ugly, and aside from a scar that ran from underneath her left eye to her nose, she was actually pretty. Now, more than anything, I wanted to mess up those delicate features.

"No?" she continued, one of her eyebrows arching up in a mocking gesture. "That's a shame. Are you *his* pet, then?"

"Shut up with that bullshit already." I tried to take

one step toward her, but two men immediately grabbed me by the shoulders and forced me to remain in place. "Just what do you think you're going to accomplish by coming down here? Can't you see that you're making everything worse?"

"Am I?" she scoffed. "So you're telling me that when your friends came onto the planet, unleashing war and God knows what else upon all of us, that things were just peachy? Because that's not how I remember it."

"And do you think that by messing with the Puppet Master you'll make things better somehow?"

"Puppet Master, right, that's what you call it," she laughed. "A rather silly name, don't you think? Anyway, none of that matters. And you're right—I'm going to make things better for everyone. You just watch. I'm going to usher in a new age."

"You're out of your goddamn mind."

"Maybe," she shrugged. "But at least I'm fighting for us humans. As for you..."

She looked into my eyes, gave me a pitying smile, and glanced at Sa'lok before shaking her head in a disappointed manner.

Turning her back to me, she headed toward the rest of her group and whispered something to one of the men. He clapped his hands together, the sound of it filling the entire chamber, and a couple of seconds later, three more men stepped out from the darkened mouth of a secondary tunnel.

"Careful," Amenya said, but the sound of her voice was drowned out by a rabid growl. Turning my head, I watched as the newcomers dragged a middle-aged man toward the center of the chamber.

He was bare-chested, and he had an unkempt and ragged appearance. There were bruises all over his chest, and his wrists had not been bound with rope, but with metal handcuffs.

Although his appearance was human, the light behind his eyes betrayed what he really was: one of the infected.

He was growling through gritted teeth, his chin wet with drool. He kept on pushing his wrists against the handcuffs, fighting hard to break them, and it took three grown men to stop him from thrashing around.

Under Amenya's supervising gaze, they dragged the possessed one near the Puppet Master's core, and only then did I realize what these idiots were trying to do.

"Are you idiots out of your mind?" Sa'lok growled, his eyes burning with fury. He had seen it, too. "Do you have any idea what you're doing?"

"I didn't know that beasts were capable of speech," Amenya merely said. I thought that she was going to ignore Sa'lok, but she didn't.

She took a couple of steps toward him, then

slammed the butt of her rifle in his stomach, doing it so hard that he actually went down on one knee, despite the protection of his skinsuit.

"Keep quiet, or your friend will pay the price." With that, she turned her attention back to what was happening near the Puppet Master. "Do it now."

At once, the men held the possessed one by the hair and rammed his face against the outer shell of the Puppet Master's core.

The man thrashed for a moment, trying to break free from his captors, but then he straightened his back and stopped moving altogether, his body going rigid.

"What the hell...?" I muttered under my breath, not exactly sure what I was seeing. The infected started swaying back and forth on his heels, as if he was lost in a trance, then he suddenly fell to the floor.

The three men around him jumped back, as if knowing what was going to happen, and the man started seizing.

When he started foaming at the mouth, the anti-alien guys hoisted him to his feet and went back to pressing him against the Puppet Master's core.

From where I was standing, I couldn't see how they were doing it, but there was no doubt in my mind of *what* was happening: the Gorgo inside the infected human was seeping out from its human host and into the Puppet Master.

"Stop it!" I yelled out, but that just earned me a backhanded slap across my face.

"I told you I'd kill you all if you touched her," Sa'lok shouted, his words seething with anger, and then he threw his head back.

A fraction of a second later, he rammed his forehead against the nose of the man standing in front of him.

Half a dozen of them started rushing toward Sa'lok, determined to kick the shit out of him, but they all froze in their tracks when the vines strewn across the floor, all of them limp and lifeless, suddenly started to move.

I threw myself to the floor and narrowly avoided being hit, as one of them whipped the place where my head had been.

The tendrils were moving in a frenzy, no logic to their movements, and the vines were hitting everything they could—from men to the walls, everything was fair game.

The Puppet Master was struggling against them with everything he had.

But in his fight against the Gorgos, he might destroy us all.

Rolling to the side, I watched as everyone in the cave started running around like headless chickens.

Apparently they hadn't been expecting such a

reaction out of the Puppet Master, and they had no idea how to stop it.

"Oh, crap," I whispered as I saw thick vines breaking through the rocky ground, more of them coming out from the ceiling.

Clouds of dust started taking over all the empty space, and it only took a couple of seconds before I started hearing the rumble of stones coming loose.

"Shit, shit, shit," I kept on repeating, pushing myself across the floor with nothing but my heels. Large stones were already falling from the ceiling, and soon enough the entire chamber would cave.

"Teisha!" I heard Sa'luk shout, but by then it was already too late.

The last thing I saw was a crack cutting across the domed ceiling, and the loud sound of it coming apart.

Then, there was only darkness.

SA'LOK

My head hurt.

Still with my eyes closed, I rolled to my back and coughed, my lungs and stomach feeling as if someone had poured a cup of dust down my throat.

Silently, I ordered a diagnostic routine to begin.

Nothing broken. That was a good start.

I sat up, my body sore. I felt the jagged contour of the rubble underneath me biting into my muscles. When I finally opened my eyes, it took me a couple of seconds before I realized where I was.

The Puppet Master's chamber, a spacious cavern with a domed ceiling and smooth walls, stalactites and stalagmites all around, had become nothing but a gigantic pile of rubble. Pieces of broken rocks lay all around, the rubble covering the ground like a monstrous carpet of chaos, and a thick cloud of dust still hung in the air, irritating my lungs.

Teisha, I suddenly remembered, that one thought welling up in my mind like a bright neon sign. I jumped to my feet as panic took hold of me and, disoriented, I started looking around for any sign of her. I headed straight toward the last place where I saw her, and my stomach lurched as I saw only a massive cracked boulder there.

My blood ran cold and I closed my eyes and took a deep breath. *Keep it together, Sa'lok.*

Focusing on one problem at a time, I decided to deal with the rope around my wrists before I tried doing anything else. Going down on my knees, I grabbed a small sharp rock and started cutting through the rope. It took me a couple of minutes before I managed to cut through.

Rubbing my wrists, I looked down at them to see my skin was red and irritated despite the skin suit; those anti-alien assholes had tightened the rope so much that I was pretty sure I'd be left with a couple of bruises, and maybe some raw skin.

Groaning, I went back to my feet and immediately tried to move the boulder resting on the place where I had last seen Teisha.

I wanted to call to her, but there was no way for me to know how many of the enemy may have survived.

If we were going to get out of here, stealth was the only way.

My muscles tensed from the effort and beads of sweat trickled down my forehead as I pushed, flooding my system with adrenaline to increase my strength.

It would cost me later, but I'd gladly pay the price. I had to find Teisha.

I let out a muffled scream as the boulder finally started to move. My heart was drumming anxiously and the palms of my hands were damp with sweat as, for a second, I imagined Teisha's body crushed between the ground and the merciless rock.

But she wasn't there.

Breathing a sigh of relief, I started looking around once more. The dust made it hard to see anything, but I immediately noticed a few lifeless bodies underneath the rubble, dirty boots and twisted limbs sticking out from the dirt.

Hoping that Teisha wasn't among them, I started pulling on every rock I could find, my heart beating faster and faster with each passing second.

Where the hell *was* she?

Suddenly, I heard someone coughing from a few feet behind me. I spun around as fast as I could, adrenaline kicking in again as I saw a female human shape lying underneath a blanket of rocks and dirt.

Pushing the rocks away, thankfully none of them

larger than my fist, I uncovered Teisha and gently pulled her against me.

She was unconscious, but still breathing. Patting the sides of her body, I carefully looked her over to see if I could spot any major injuries. She'd have a lot of bruises, I had no doubts about it, but aside from that, she seemed to be alright. I closed my eyes for a second and breathed in, doing my best to steady my nerves. Had something happened to her, I would've never forgiven myself.

Gently, I picked her up from the floor and started walking toward the edge of the cavern. Finding a spot that had been left miraculously untouched by the cave-in, I sat Teisha there and leaned her back against the smooth wall.

"Teisha," I whispered, stroking her cheek with the back of my hand. "Can you hear me?" Her eyes moved underneath her eyelids, but her body remained perfectly still.

Her chest rose and fell at a steady pace, though, and that gave me some ease of mind. Sitting down next to her, I looked at my own body for the first time since regaining consciousness.

I had a few bloody cuts on my arms, and my knees were scuffed, but aside from the soreness in my muscles, I felt fine. Resting my elbows on my knees, I looked at the destruction in the cavern, the dust making it impossible for me to see more than ten feet ahead.

But even though I couldn't see, I could still hear the dazed voices coming from the other side of the chamber.

Apparently, Teisha and I hadn't been the only survivors.

"I'll be right back," I whispered, and pressed a kiss to her forehead. Just to reassure her.

Really.

Crawling away from Teisha as silently as I could, I scanned my surroundings until I found what I was looking for—my rifle lay underneath a few loose stones and, aside from a couple of dents, it didn't seem to be broken.

Grabbing it, I checked if it was in working order and turned the safety off. I fleetingly thought of activating the stun mode, which would make the rifle use chemically enhanced darts that would knock anyone unconscious, but quickly discarded the idea.

I had made a promise to these assholes and, unless they surrendered, I intended to keep it.

Crouching, I held my breath and started moving through the dust as silently as I could. It took me almost a minute to get to the other end of the cavern, but once I got there, I immediately saw human shapes moving in the distance.

Drawing close, I waited until they realized I was standing next to them, then fired at their feet. The sound of it echoed throughout the cavern, and the five surviving assholes jumped back from the scare.

"Don't move," I growled, advancing toward them, "or I'll put a hole in each and every one of you."

"You survived," one of the humans coughed, and I recognized the voice as belonging to Amenya, the group leader.

She was leaning against the wall, her brown hair covered in dust, and blood was trickling down her forehead. She was grinning. "You're a tough one, aren't you?"

"Why are you doing this?" I asked, pointing my rifle at her. "Have you lost your mind?"

"Am I the one who unleashed hell upon our cities?" she replied, her words brimming with spite. Sneering, she spat at my feet. "You brought death to our doorstep."

"I didn't—"

"You brought chaos and destruction," she continued, cutting me short. "You pulled us into your war against the Xathi, and now you're dragging us into war again. I'm not going to allow it."

"What are you talking about?" I growled. "You're not going to stop the Gorgos like this."

"Stop them?" she laughed, sounding almost

hysterical. Pushing herself off the wall, she took a couple of steps toward me. "Who said anything about stopping them? The Gorgoxians are going to wipe the floor with you. You think you can stand up to them? You're an idiot. The Gorgoxians are here to stay."

Suddenly, it all made sense.

These idiots had brokered a deal with the Gorgos. They were no longer focusing on human rule and kicking the aliens out—they had bent the knee to what they saw as their new overlords.

"Are you stupid?" Gritting my teeth, I put my finger on the trigger. "You're working with them?"

"Is there any use in fighting against them?" Shrugging, she took one more step toward me. "We do that, and we're all going to be infected in a couple of weeks. But *we* were offered mercy. We were offered our planet back, and the only thing we had to do was get rid of your beloved Puppet Master's defenses."

"You're a fucking idiot," I growled. "You have no idea what you've just done."

"Am I really the idiot here?" she continued, a grin spreading across her lips. Walking straight toward me, she only stopped when she had the muzzle of my rifle pressed against her chest. "Maybe you're right. But at least I'm going to be alive. As for you..."

Faster than I had expected, she grabbed my rifle and pushed it to the side.

I was already starting to lag from the adrenaline dump. Skrell.

I squeezed the trigger, but she had already stepped to the opposite side, and so my shot merely ricocheted off the wall.

"Die," she spat, ducking underneath my rifle and reaching for something in her boot. I saw the clear glint of a blade, but it was already too late.

Even though I tried to jump back, she slashed at me, cutting through my shirt. I felt the blade's serrated edge burn against my skin, tearing a jagged line through my skin-suit and circuitry.

"No," I said through gritted teeth. "*You* die." I flooded my system with another round of adrenaline and kicked her right in the chest, sending her tumbling to the ground.

She hissed like a snake, readying herself to jump toward me, and I heard the shuffling of boots as the remaining four survivors started circling me. With no other choice, I squeezed the trigger and shot Amenya right in the forehead.

"You alien scum," one of the men screamed, throwing himself on top of my rifle. I shot him in the chest, but he still managed to yank the rifle out of my hands as he collapsed to the floor.

Two of the other men immediately moved in, grabbing me by the arms and pinning me against the wall, while the remaining one went for my gun.

He spun around so that he was aiming at me, a victorious grin on his face, and squeezed the trigger.

Nothing happened.

"What the fuck?" he cried, and took his finger from the trigger, to see a drop of blood trickling down from a small cut. Then, just a fraction of a second later, he swayed like a drunkard and fell back.

"No one but me can fire it," I grinned. "You've just been poisoned."

"You're going to pay for this," one of the men that was holding me threatened, but I simply pushed both my arms down and forced them to let go of me. Even though they were using all their strength, they were no match for me with my system turned all the way up.

Turning on my heels, I grabbed one by the collar of his shirt and pulled him toward me as fast as I could, my forehead on a collision course with his nose. The moment I hit him, he folded like a house of cards knocked over by the wind.

The remaining one tried to escape from me in a hurry, scrabbling through the rubble on all fours, but I grabbed him and slammed him against the wall.

I pushed him up until his feet were no longer touching the floor, his eyes now level with mine, and I recognized the man that had slapped Teisha before.

"Please, no, don't—"

"I told you," I hissed. "You touch her, you're dead."

"Oh, God, no, please—" As he spoke, I noticed him trying to reach for a knife that hung from his belt. Before he could pull it free, I cocked my arm back and punched him with all my strength, forcing his neck to snap back.

His body went limp at once, and I let it drop.

Breathing hard, I wiped the sweat off my brow as I tried to regain my bearings. Then, as if to ground me to reality, I heard a faint voice echoing throughout the cavern.

"Sa'lok?" Teisha called weakly. "Where are you?"

TEISHA

Relief washed over me once I saw the outline of Sa'lok's hulking body moving through the thick clouds of dust. I leaned back against the wall and breathed out, raking one hand over my dirty face.

"I thought you had..." I trailed off, unable to complete my sentence. I had always taken Sa'lok for granted, and only now that I had been forced to contemplate an existence without him did I realize how much that would hurt.

I needed him in my life.

Shock ran through me as I realized how *much* I needed him. "Are you okay?" I stumbled over my words, trying not to betray myself.

"I'm fine," he said, but I immediately noticed a long

gash showing under his ripped shirt. It didn't look like that had been caused by the cave-in.

No, that was the work of a very sharp knife.

"Where are those bastards? Did any of them survive?"

"Some of them did," he replied, "but they won't be a problem, not anymore."

I just nodded at that. I didn't need him to explain what had happened. All I needed to know was that he was alright.

"What about the Puppet Master?"

"I don't know," he admitted, pursing his lips. He clenched his fists tightly, and his bloody knuckles started going white. "I've been to the other side of the chamber and back, but this place is a mess. It's impossible to get to the center and see how the Puppet Master is. At least not without any heavy machinery or tools."

"But we have to try and—" I groaned as I got to my feet, pain shooting through my shoulder. Grimacing, I placed one hand on it and realized I had dislocated it. "Oh, crap."

"Is it broken?"

"No," I shook my head, "I don't think so, just dislocated."

"I can help." Standing behind me, Sa'lok pressed his

body against mine and I held my breath, his closeness almost intoxicating.

I closed my eyes as I felt his large hands on me, his touch soft and gentle, and my mind started spiraling out of control. I imagined how it would feel to have his hands wandering all over my naked skin, and I— "Holy shit," I cried out, my bones popping back into place as Sa'lok applied just the right amount of pressure on my shoulder.

"Better now?"

"Yeah, I think so," I replied, hesitantly rotating my arm. My shoulder felt sore, but functional. The moment Sa'lok let go of me, though, I almost fell over.

My right ankle struggled with my full weight, and if weren't for Sa'lok's quick reaction, I would have fallen face first to the floor.

"Careful," he said, both his hands on my hips. "You must've sprained your ankle, as well."

"Looks like it, yeah," I muttered, while at the same time, a loud sound echoed throughout the chaotic chamber, like stones grinding together.

"It isn't safe here." With one hand wrapped around my waist, Sa'lok carefully adjusted my left arm and draped it over his shoulders. "We have to leave before there's another cave-in."

"But the Puppet Master—"

"There's nothing we can do right now, Teisha." He

shook his head. "We have to leave and let the general know about what's happening. These anti-alien guys brokered a deal with the Gorgos, and the Puppet Master might be dead or infected. We need to act fast before the Gorgoxians go on the offensive."

"Fine," I relented. It felt like giving up, but Sa'lok was right. There was nothing left for us to do here. Using him as my support, I limped toward the one tunnel mouth that hadn't been covered by all the falling rock. "Do you know the way out?"

"Not through this specific tunnel, but we'll figure something out."

"Right," I nodded. I didn't know if getting lost in a maze of caves and tunnels and dying of thirst would be much better than dying in a cave-in, but I said nothing else and continued down the sloping tunnel, my flashlight struggling to keep the darkness at bay.

After half an hour of walking, we finally sat down to catch our breaths. The backup team the general had sent was probably already making their way through the tunnels, which was good, but we didn't have any way of reaching them—Sa'lok's comms unit had been destroyed during the cave-in, which meant right now we were cut off from the rest of the world.

When it was finally time for us to stand up, I noticed something out of the corner of my eye.

It was a small vine tendril lying on the ground,

hidden by an outcrop of jagged rocks. "Look," I cried, elbowing Sa'lok while I pointed at the vine. Before he had any time to say something, I limped toward it and kneeled next to it.

I exchanged a glance with Sa'lok, then he reached for the plant with the tips of his fingers.

"I don't feel anything."

My heart sunk as he said it, but I still reached for the vine all the same. I wrapped my fingers around it and, just like Sa'lok had said, I didn't feel a thing. The Puppet Master's presence had faded.

"Do you think the Puppet Master has—?" I stopped speaking as the vine gently started moving, coiling itself around my wrist.

Its movements were heavy and slow, almost as if whatever force was inhabiting it was starting to fade, but it was a positive sign, all the same.

"No, I don't think he is," Sa'lok replied, never looking away from the vine as it moved. "But he's not speaking, either, is he?"

"No, he isn't," I agreed. Closing my eyes, I tried to still my mind and attempted to feel the Puppet Master's presence one last time.

For a fraction of a second, I thought I felt something faint and tenuous in the distance, but it could be just my imagination. "What do we do, Sa'lok?"

"I have no idea." It was slightly disconcerting to see a

guy like him admit that he was at a loss, but I didn't blame him. I also had no idea what we should do. "We'll update the general on what happened, and then go from there."

"If we manage to get out of here alive," I added, but quickly regretted saying it. I only meant it as a joke, but Sa'lok's exhausted expression told me he was considering my words as a real possibility. Great.

Thankfully, his mood brightened after a couple more minutes of walking.

"I think I recognize this place," he said, arms folded over his chest as he peered at the walls of the tunnel we were in. "I've been through here before. I think that if we make the next left turn, we'll be on our way out of here."

Turned out, he was right. We made a left turn, walked for twenty minutes, and came across the rescue party the general had sent, a burly Skotan I didn't recognize leading them.

"No use in pushing ahead," Sa'lok told them. "The main chamber has caved in. If you guys want to go in there and look around, you better have some machinery with you. Just get us out of here."

No one bothered arguing with him. Two members of the search team split off to secure the chamber, and the rest of us trooped along the tunnel in a single file.

A few minutes later, we were stepping outside, the bright afternoon sun baking everything underneath it.

"Where to?" the team leader asked Sa'lok, and his response was a prompt one.

"Nyheim," he said wearily. "I need to speak with the general."

SA'LOK

Teisha fell asleep shortly after we took off. Her tired body was leaning against mine, her head resting on my shoulder. Dust and small pieces of debris were covering her disheveled hair, but I thought she looked beautiful, all the same.

Tired and exhausted, too, but those things did little to diminish her beauty.

"Rest," I whispered, even though I knew she couldn't hear me, and draped one arm around her shoulders.

The letdown from the adrenaline dump couldn't be pushed off any further without risking damage to my systems.

We were safe now, I reminded myself.

Through the window, I watched the desert

underneath us turning into a blur as the aerial units zoomed through the skies, wisps of clouds lining the way ahead. Two ships were escorting ours, while the remaining two and their occupants had remained behind to ensure no one else would try to get back into the tunnels.

I closed my eyes and finally allowed exhaustion to embrace my worn muscles. The bruises I had all over my body were tender spots of flesh that had started turning blue, and my forearms and stomach were covered in caked blood. Some of it was mine, some wasn't.

It didn't take long before I drifted off, the steady rumble of the engines lulling me into sleep. I dreamed of the Puppet Master, its honest and caring voice replaced by hollow silence, and I dreamed of the Gorgos and the possessed.

I saw the possessed ravaging the countryside, hordes of furious figures claiming the planet as their own as they advanced upon the cities and their prey.

"Are you alright?" A soft voice cut through my dreams, and I felt delicate fingers grasping my arm. Opening my eyes, I turned to the side to find Teisha staring at me, her eyes two round pools of lively green. "You were talking in your sleep."

"Sorry." Laying my hand on top of hers, I gave it a squeeze. "I can't stop my mind from racing."

"Are you worried?"

"Not exactly," I lied. "We're gonna figure something out. We always do." She saw through my lie easily enough, but she didn't say anything. She was worried, too, probably thinking of her sister and her nephew and niece.

Away from a well-guarded city like Nyheim, they were probably more vulnerable to a Gorgo attack than anyone else. Then again, who could be sure?

As far as I knew, the Gorgos would focus on laying waste to the cities first. There was just no way of knowing what was going through their ancient minds.

"We're landing in five," the Skotan pilot announced over the comms, and Teisha rested her head against my chest once more. This time she was awake, though, her alert eyes looking out the window and taking in the city.

Nyheim's tall glass towers glinted under the afternoon sun, and even from a distance, I could see the chaotic air traffic enveloping the city. Slowly but steadily, the city was recovering from the war against the Xathi, a sense of normalcy finally returning to it.

I didn't know if that would last.

We landed in a secluded part of the hangar, and I immediately spotted the general waiting for us near the landing pad. His usual retinue of aides and assistants wasn't around, and his expression was a stern one.

He stood with his back straight, hands folded behind his back, and his crisp military uniform—a blend of human traditions and those we followed aboard the *Vengeance*—gave him the look of a man that was ready to wage war by himself.

"Sa'lok," he said, clasping my forearm in a warrior's salute. "I'm glad to see that you're alive and breathing." His eyes darted to the wounds covering both my arms and stomach, and I uncomfortably shifted my weight from one foot to the other. "I've already heard a simplified version of what happened, but I wanted to hear it directly from you. Is it true that we've lost contact with the Puppet Master?"

"Yes," I nodded. "I don't believe that he's dead, but he's not communicating, either. The anti-alien faction that we faced in the tunnels tried to infect him with a Gorgo, but I don't know if they were successful. There was a cave-in and—"

"I'm aware," General Rouhr nodded gravely. "You gave me a lot to think about, Sa'lok. I want to hear the full details of what happened first thing tomorrow morning, but right now I want the two of you to get checked out at the med bay." He glanced at Teisha and smiled. "You did well."

"Thank you, General," Teisha and I said in unison.

"Evie's already expecting you," he finished. "Don't make her wait. You know how she gets."

With that, he was gone, walking across the hangar with his head bowed and his hands clasped behind his back.

Not knowing what else to do, I led Teisha out of the hangar and into the main building, navigating my way through the floors until I saw the clear doors of the med bay.

Evie, a young woman wearing a white coat, stood in the doorway with her arms folded over her chest. Her auburn hair had been pulled back into a ponytail, and her blue eyes shone with frustration.

One of the most capable doctors in the building, she had been the first human to establish contact with the Urai, and one of the first to deal with the hybrid epidemic that ravaged the continent during the Xathi invasion.

"What is it with you people?" she sighed, shaking her head in a disapproving manner. "There's always someone getting stuck in ruins, caves, and tunnels. It's as if you people don't like being out on the surface."

Deciding to move forward without any kind of small talk, she led the way into a small room inside the med bay and told Teisha and me to sit on opposite stretchers. "The only reason my bay's full all the time is because you people just *have* to go underground, no matter how stupid or dangerous it is."

"It's part of the job," I shrugged, and Evie gave me a resigned shake of her head.

"That's what Sakev keeps telling me," she sighed. During the Xathi war, she had grown close to Sakev, a heavy-hitter on Vrehx's strike team, and to everyone's surprise, they'd become mates. "You ask me, you guys hide behind 'duty' to go out and blow things up."

"That's a fair assessment," I laughed, but my laugh was immediately replaced by a groan as Evie started stitching up the wound on my stomach.

"Deep down, they're just boys," Teisha added with a laugh of her own, and the two women exchanged a knowing glance. Even though I didn't think they had met before, I could tell these two would get along well if given the chance.

"You, go get into the repair unit for the damage to your components while I fix up your friend here," Evie ordered me. "Move fast, or I'll tell her how to deactivate you."

Half an hour later, Evie was discharging us. She pushed us out of the room with warnings to 'have a couple of days off' and 'be more careful next time', then ushered her next patients in with a quick wave of her hand.

"She's intense," Teisha said as we walked out of the med bay. "I like her."

"I thought you would."

I kept on walking down the hallway that led to the teams' quarters when I suddenly realized that Teisha probably didn't have a place in the city where she could stay. She didn't say a thing about it, though, and I immediately realized what her plan was. "You're not thinking of flying back home today, are you?"

"Of course I am," she shrugged. "I asked one of the guys from the strike team that retrieved us to tow my hovercraft in. It should be here before night falls."

"No way." My voice came out more sternly than I had intended, but I pushed through, all the same. "I'm not going to let you fly like this. You're all banged up, and you're exhausted. You need a good night's rest before you even start thinking of stepping foot inside a hangar."

Her shoulders sagged.

"Fine, you're right," she sighed, to my surprise. Teisha never accepted my suggestions this easily, especially when it came to flying.

She had to be dead tired. "I'll see if I can book a hotel room nearby, and then I—"

"Nonsense," I cut her short. "My quarters are just around the corner. You can spend the night there." I looked at her just in time to see her green eyes widen with...*something*. I couldn't exactly tell what was going through her mind, but I noticed the way her cheeks started turning a pale shade of red.

We didn't say anything as we walked toward my room, and only when we stepped inside it did I notice there was a problem with my idea: there was only the one bed.

Normally, I wouldn't even have had that. For years, I'd slept in a maintenance chair, like most K'ver.

But since we'd been on this planet, we'd advanced the technology, making it smaller and able to be integrated into small field devices.

Now, instead of needing the bulky chairs, every K'ver could choose to sleep on whatever surface was convenient.

Given my fascination with humans, I'd been curious to try sleeping in a bed, but it took up so much of the room, I hadn't been able to fit much other furniture into the small room.

I'd never thought much about it before.

Of course, I'd never had anyone else staying over before, either.

Maybe I should have kept the chair, and then I'd have the bed to offer Teisha.

Too late now.

"Are you trying to trick a defenseless damsel, Sa'lok?" Teisha laughed, punching my arm while she cocked one eyebrow up. "You're a rascal, aren't you?"

"It's nothing like that," I hurried to say, and now it was my turn to feel blood rushing to my cheeks. "You take the bed and I'll just sleep on the floor. Honestly, it's not that much different than a basic maintenance chair."

She shook her head. "I'm tired enough I'm not even going to argue." She gave me a slight smile, then walked past me toward the bathroom. "I'm just gonna take a shower, alright?"

"Of course. I'll set some spare clothing out for you." I shrugged. "They'll be too big, but they'll be clean."

"Sounds heavenly, but no peeking," she called over her shoulder.

"Of course not," I said, but once I started hearing the sound of the running water, my mind immediately started imagining every single curve of Teisha's naked body. In my mind's eye, I saw the warm water cascaded down her petite body, caressing her breasts and hips, and my body started heating up.

When she finally emerged from the bathroom, a white towel wrapped around her body, I could no longer think straight. She stood in the doorway, hands on her hips, and gave me a questioning glance.

"No clothing?"

"What?" For a moment I couldn't think of what she was talking about. "Oh, right."

"Why are you looking at me like that?" she asked me,

but the little smile that was tugging at the corners of her lips told me she already knew the answer. "You keep on looking at me like that, and you might burn away my towel."

"Would that be such a bad thing?" I found myself saying, my heart pumping so hard I couldn't even hear my own thoughts.

More than anything, I wanted to go up to her and kiss her cherry lips. To pin her against the wall and feel her body under mine, her fingernails clawing at my back. To stop that from happening, I looked away from her and down at my feet.

"Sa'lok...Is there something wrong?"

"You know, when I woke up in the cavern and didn't see you anywhere...I thought I had lost you," I admitted, finally looking up into her eyes once more. "And it hurt. It really did."

Slowly, I took one step toward her. This time, she didn't tease me or come up with some silly joke.

She just watched me close the distance between us, her green eyes reflecting the dim light of the room, her lips slightly parted. Why did she have to be so beautiful? "It was then that I realized...this planet is worth saving because you're on it, Teisha."

"I don't even know what to say to that," she whispered.

"I'm sorry. Maybe I shouldn't have—"

She didn't let me finish. Taking one step forward, she went on her tiptoes and crushed her mouth against mine.

TEISHA

In the end, Sa'lok didn't sleep on the floor.

We cuddled under the sheets, our bodies pressed together in the darkness, but exhaustion got the best of us.

I arched under his caressing hands, but far too soon, he pulled me tight against his side.

"You're exhausted, Teisha. You need to sleep."

"I need something else," I argued, letting my hand drift down his side until it brushed against something impossibly hard and thick.

He gently pulled my hand back and rolled us until his broad chest curled against my back, my arms crossed in front of me.

"I'd be happy to give you everything you need," he

murmured into my hair, "just as soon as we both get some rest."

I wanted to argue, but a soft comfortable mattress, the warmth of a comfortable quilt, and the arms of a strong man around me—that recipe was enough to knock me out until the alarm clock rang, the pink glow of a rising sun filtering through the curtains of Sa'lok's cramped bedroom.

And then there'd been the summons to report to General Rouhr, and everything else had been a rush.

That had been hours ago, but I could still feel the warmth of Sa'lok's naked chest under the palms of my hands, that pleasant feeling lingering on my fingertips. God, what I wouldn't give to be back under the covers with him right now.

"Anything else, Teisha?" the general asked, drumming his fingers against the edge of his desk. He was looking straight at me, his eyebrows arched in a curious expression. I had already finished my report, but instead of sitting back down, I had allowed my mind to wander and simply stood in front of the general's desk like an idiot.

Smiling, I shook my head and looked around the packed office. Despite how busy everyone was, the general had insisted that all the strike team leaders be present during our retelling of events. I knew most of them from my stint as a pilot during the Xathi war, but

I couldn't remember the last time I had seen every single one of them crammed inside a room. Clearly, the general was prioritizing this situation over anything else.

There were others, too. The women in the room I recognized as Maki and Alessa, the archeologist in charge of the original dig site and the engineer tasked with digging them up, and Leena, a renowned geneticist that had been part of the war effort.

I'd looked around for Mariella, but oddly, she wasn't there.

As for the rest of the aliens, a mix of Skotan and K'ver soldiers, I had only seen in passing, and couldn't put names to their faces.

"First things first," the general said as I took my seat. Leaning back, he looked around the room and focused on Sa'lok, who was sitting right beside me. "As you've told us, the Puppet Master has destroyed the only vial you had with a cure. That particular serum is gone, but do you think you can reengineer it?"

"I should be able to," Sa'lok admitted. "I wasn't exactly following protocol and noting everything down, as we were in a hurry to get things done, but do I remember the formula I used. A few tweaks here and there, and I should be able to produce another working batch. The formula might need some adjustments, though, at least when it comes to enzymatic activity, but I—"

"That's good," the general said, raising the palm of his hand, cutting Sa'lok short. Even though Leena seemed to be on the edge of her seat, drinking up every single one of Sa'lok's words, the general didn't seem that interested in the scientific details. His mind was set on the big picture. "What about the Puppet Master? I know we have nothing but guesswork right now, but you were there when it happened. Do you think the Puppet Master has succumbed to the Gorgos?"

There was a moment of silence, one that seemed to weigh on everyone's shoulders. Sa'lok leaned forward and lowered his voice, and the team leaders standing behind him seemed to be holding their breath.

"I don't know," Sa'lok shook his head. "We saw the anti-alien faction force a foaming Gorgo onto the Puppet Master, but I believe he tried to resist it. In any case, I don't think that was the first Gorgo they'd tried to infect him with. Judging by the fact he tried to destroy the serum, back when Teisha and I were still in the lab, I'd say they had already tried doing it before."

"You think it would take more than just one Gorgo to infect him?"

"It's likely." Nodding, Sa'lok cleared his throat before continuing. "The Puppet Master is very different from a human being, and he's far more powerful than anyone or anything else. The Gorgo will have a hard time subduing him. The fact that he's not reaching out leads me to believe he has been infected, yes, but his immune system—for lack of a better term—is probably trying to fight it off."

There was a pause, then Sa'lok leaned back in his seat. "But if we don't do something, and do it soon...then I believe the Puppet Master will be done for." Even though no one said a word, it was obvious the exact same question burned in everyone's minds— we had to do something, no doubt about it, but *what?*

Alessa was the first one to speak.

"Maybe I could redirect my team from the dig site," she started. "We could head into the Puppet Master's lair and try to dig through. You said there was a cave-in on the main chamber, but if his core is still there—"

"Don't bother with it," Vrehx stepped forward, his lips pursed tightly. "My team has already been there. There's no sign of the Puppet Master anywhere. More likely than not, the core has gone underground. If we try to dig through, we might end up—"

"Causing more damage, yeah," Alessa sighed. "Message received."

The back-and-forth between the crowd assembled inside the general's office continued for the better part of an hour, but a clear path of action remained outside our reach.

The Gorgos had played their pieces perfectly by enlisting those xenophobic bastards to their cause, and now our backs were against the wall.

Our strongest ally had been removed from the chessboard, and we had no idea what the enemy was planning.

As a pilot, that immediately made me think of someone flying blind after his main engine had blown up. Not a good scenario.

"Let's focus on the anti-alien factions for a moment," Sa'lok said, raising his voice just so he could make himself heard. By now, everyone was talking at the same time, frustration getting the best of the room. "We have a lot of their members under surveillance. Maybe we can bring some of them in for questioning and—"

He was silenced by the sound of the office door swinging back on its hinges and hitting the wall as someone burst into the room.

We all turned around to see who the newcomer was, some of the Skotans automatically reaching for their rifles, but they immediately relaxed.

Mariella stood in the doorway, her disheveled hair framing her frantic expression.

"I'm sorry I was late and to barge in like this," she started, her breathing ragged. She had been running, it seemed. "But I have news."

"Let us hear it then," the general said evenly. He

didn't seem annoyed that our meeting had been interrupted. If anything, he seemed relieved. No wonder—the more we argued about what we should be doing, the more confused everyone got.

"Late last night I got word that more ruins were found near Glymna. A merchant crew had engine trouble and ended up making an emergency landing in unmarked territory." She grinned. "I suspect they may not be entirely on the up and up, but that's someone else's problem." She pulled back her hair, started braiding it as she spoke. "Going over the maps with Fen, it seems that, though the ruins were easy to access from the ground, they were surrounded by geological formations that prevented the Urai satellites from picking them up earlier. And, the best part is, there's writing everywhere."

"More writing?" Maki sighed. For an archeologist, she didn't seem too excited about the new findings. "We already have so much writing to sift through. The Aeryx writing system is complex and—"

"I'm gonna stop you right there," Mariella interrupted her, and there was a glint in her eyes. "I'm not talking about the Aeryx. I'm talking about the Gorgos."

"Hang on," Maki said. "What are you talking about?"

Taking a deep breath, Mariella straightened her back and ran her tongue over her lips. "The writing we found is different," she replied, her tone now more controlled than before. "Very, very different. Fen believes it belongs to the Gorgos." She looked around the room with wide eyes. "We came across their writing system."

Now *that* got the room's interest.

SA'LOK

Not surprisingly, the meeting broke into chaos, everyone talking at once.

Mariella left just ahead of Maki and Teisha, and I brought up the rear, closing the office door as I left.

"Are you absolutely sure we're talking about the Gorgos?" Maki asked, upping her pace so that she was walking beside Mariella. "According to what I've seen, the Aeryx system has a lot of thematic variations. The script seems to change whenever the theme changes. It's highly possible you've come across one of those variations."

"I'm not the one who's saying these runes don't belong to the Aeryx," Mariella said, glancing at Maki as a smile spread across her face. "Fen and her team are the ones who are convinced. And I don't really think of her as a gambling kind of person."

"The Urai said that?" Maki repeated, and it was obvious that Mariella had finally managed to convince the archeologist of the finding's relevance.

She started walking faster now, as if she couldn't wait to dive into all the new material that had been uncovered.

"Here we are," Mariella announced, swiping the card that hung from her neck across a small panel. The sealed door in front of us hissed for a couple of seconds, and then it swung back lazily.

The labs were similar to what we had used in Glymna, but the rooms were cramped and stuffy. Mariella didn't seem bothered by that. She took a sharp turn left and stepped inside the largest room on the floor, the walls made of thick floor-to-ceiling glass panels.

At the center of the room was a large circular table, hundreds of pictures strewn across its surface.

Without waiting for Mariella's say-so, Teisha made a beeline straight toward the table. Placing the palm of both her hands on the edge of it, she leaned forward and scanned all the documents in front of her with one quick glance.

"This is impressive," she muttered, her eyes wide with excitement. Standing beside her, I looked down at the table to see pictures of runes etched on ancient walls.

Their lines were sharp and angular, and there was a kind of roughness to the script.

I wouldn't exactly call what I was seeing an impressive thing, but what did I know?

I wasn't the archeologist or the linguist.

"Even if it is the Gorgos' writing, though, where is it going to get us?" Maki asked.

Just like me, she didn't seem particularly impressed by Mariella's finding.

"If we manage to translate this," Mariella replied, tapping one of the pictures in front of her with two fingers, "then we might have a shot at deciphering the Gorgoxians' inner workings. All that we have so far are second-hand accounts of who they are and what they want, and ravings from some of the possessed. Nothing from the original species."

"They're assholes who wants us dead," Maki shrugged. "Isn't that enough?" When the two other women didn't reply, clearly not impressed with her sense of humor, she merely shrugged.

"This is where we found all this," Mariella continued, pushing a couple of pictures toward the center of the table. One was an aerial shot of the jungle that encircled Glymna and, even though it didn't pop out right away, a closer look revealed some kind of structure hiding beneath the green canopy.

The other picture had been taken from the ground and it revealed the structure's main entrance, thick stone pillars with runes etched all around them, and narrow stairs that seemed to dive straight into the ground.

"This looks similar to the temple Amira and Dax discovered a couple of months ago," Maki mused, narrowing her eyes as she analyzed the pictures. "There are some architectural differences, but the similarities are too obvious to ignore."

"Agreed," I pitched in.

Even though I hadn't been part of the investigation into all those ruins and temples, I had read all the reports and seen the pictures. Just like Maki had pointed out, the similarities were there.

"So, the Urai have already started analyzing the bulk of what we have," Mariella continued.

She was more interested in the runes themselves than any architectural analysis. "They've analyzed and transcribed snippets of what we've found, and they're pretty confident that the writing system we're seeing here has nothing to do with the one we found before."

"And have they managed to translate any of this?" I asked, waving my hand at all the pictures. The way

Mariella's lips turned downward told me the answer before she even opened her mouth.

"Not exactly," she admitted. "They've been trying to translate it with some old references they have, but all the sources they're working from are second-hand material, coming from all over the universe. According to what they've told us, it's difficult to piece together a coherent picture of the language."

"That isn't exactly helpful," I said, suddenly feeling deflated.

Mariella had been so excited about this that, for a moment, I'd actually thought we were making progress. As it turned out, we just had another piece of the puzzle, one we had no idea where to place. The way I saw it, we were just spinning our wheels.

"Sorry to bother you," I heard someone say right behind us, and I turned around to see Leena standing in the lab's doorway. She gave our little group a smile, and then focused her attention on me. "The meeting with the general has already ended. He told me to come see you, Sa'lok."

"Is it about the serum?"

"Yeah," she nodded, and I returned her smile.

Happy to have something other than mysterious runes and enigmas to focus on, I left the three women to puzzle over the Gorgos' script and led Leena toward the corner of the room, where a whiteboard had been set up against the wall.

Even though most scientists preferred working with holoscreens, I liked having something more tangible to work on.

"Given that there's a lot of things happening at the same time, the general asked me to start working on the serum." She sounded slightly apologetic, as if she was afraid of my reaction. She was probably thinking I wouldn't like to have someone taking the serum research away from me. I didn't really care.

Leena was one of the smartest people around, and I knew for a certainty that she'd improve on my work. "He says you'll probably have your hands full in the coming weeks, so—"

"Don't worry about it," I told her. "I'll ask the Glymna lab to send you all my documents. In the meantime, I'll give you a quick rundown of the formula I used. We only tested it once, and it was on someone that hadn't been infected, but it seemed to produce the desired results."

I omitted the part where Teisha had been the test subject. I had never worked closely with Leena, but something told me she wouldn't have approved of that.

"Alright, go for it."

"You'll basically have to produce a hormonal cocktail," I started to explain as I scribbled my formula on the whiteboard. "The key is to stimulate the brain in a way that'll elicit someone's happiest memories. That should be enough to break through the hold the Gorgo has on the mind." My marker moved fast over the board, but Leela seemed to be capturing all the information just as fast as I explained it.

"What about this?" she chimed in, grabbing the marker from my hands and scribbling a couple of notes beside my formula. "Accelerated protein breakdown might help, no?"

"You're right," I nodded, scratching my chin as I saw how her notes fit in with the rest of my formula. Just like I thought, Leena was the right person to be working on the serum.

"Perfect," she beamed, using her datapad to capture the information on the whiteboard. "Just send the documents from the Glymna lab whenever you can. I'm going to get started on this."

With that, she turned around and moved into the adjacent room, snapping her fingers at the lab assistant sitting there. He jumped from his chair and stood at attention while Leena barked her orders.

She was a petite woman, but when it came to her work, she was as ferocious as they come.

Stretching my back, I ambled back to where Teisha and the other women were. They were still hunched over all the pictures and translation documents, but they didn't seem to have reached any kind of consensus yet.

I wasn't surprised. If the Urai were stumped, did we really think we'd be able to translate any of this in a few hours?

Not really interested in the runes, I sat beside Teisha and reached for the aerial pictures of the temples. It was amazing to think that all those structures had remained untouched for millennia.

"Hang on," I muttered, shuffling the pictures of the three different dig sites in my hands. Narrowing my eyes, I spread them across the table in front of me, then glanced at the document in Maki's hands.

It was a list of all the runes that had been used in this hypothetical Gorgo script, an impenetrable alphabet of sorts. Jumping to my feet, I grabbed the document from Maki's hands and laid it above the pictures of the dig sites. "Can you see it?" I asked the three of them, frantically looking around.

"See what?" Leaning over the pictures, Mariella pursed her lips. "What are you talking about, Sa'lok? I don't see anything."

"I see it," Teisha cried out, and she, too, jumped up from her seat. Pointing at one of the runes, she tapped it a couple of times and then pointed at one of the dig sites. "Seen from above, this temple is exactly like this rune."

"That might be a coincidence," Maki muttered, but her eyes were already trying to find a match for the remaining dig sites. "Or maybe not," she continued, her words brimming with excitement. "These two runes here, they match the other dig sites."

"Finally," I grinned, "we're getting somewhere."

TEISHA

I couldn't get any sleep.

It was three in the morning and my brain was still working at high speed, weird runes and strange characters parading behind my closed eyelids in an endless procession.

I hadn't been hopeful about the translation efforts to start with, but it hadn't taken long before I became obsessed with cracking the code.

Back when I had been studying linguistics, I always achieved high marks, not because of all the studying I did, but because of the single-minded way I pursued things.

Whenever they reviewed my work, most of my teachers said it was a good thing to be obsessed, but they quickly backtracked on those observations when I shifted gears and my obsession became the open skies.

They believed I could become a renowned expert in the field, and that I was throwing it all away just because I wanted to try my hand at being a pilot.

Then the Xathi came.

And that simplified those career choices.

But things were different now. Long unused skills were popping up, as if they'd just been waiting for me to call on them.

Except now that I needed to sleep, there was a minor problem.

Whenever I closed my eyes, those damn characters and symbols insisted on floating up to my mind's surface, keeping me awake while the rest of the world slept.

To make matters worse, Leena had enlisted Sa'lok's help to oversee the lab's night shift. While I worked with Maki and Mariella, he slept. Then it was the opposite: he was up all night, overseeing the production of the serum throughout the night, and I was tossing and turning in his bed. That kiss we'd shared still lingered in my mind, and I was dying for more.

So much more.

Whenever I wasn't thinking of the Gorgos and their indecipherable alphabet, I was thinking of Sa'lok.

Sighing, I kicked the sheets back and sprawled myself on the bed. I opened my eyes and stared at the ceiling for a long time, allowing my mind to wander freely.

It was all so frustrating, but there was nothing I could do about it. Sa'lok and I were impossibly busy, and that meant whatever we felt toward each other would simply have to wait.

"Teisha, are you awake?" My comms unit crackled all of a sudden, startling me. I had the habit of muting it during the night, but I had stopped doing it once I started working with the runes, just in case something came up.

"Yeah, I'm here," I replied, swinging my legs off the bed and grabbing the comms unit. "What's up?"

"We just got a response from Fen," Maki said, and the excitement in her voice was palpable. "I've got a stack of files from her."

"Perfect." Jumping to my feet, I started getting dressed as fast as I could, not even bothering with combing my unruly hair. "I'll be there in ten," I continued, putting my boots on and rushing out of Sa'lok's bedroom.

Fen, our liaison with the Urai, had been assisting us with cracking the Gorgo script.

On a hunch, I had decided to ask Fen for a lexicon of languages that were similar to the one we were working on, and it seemed like it had finally come through.

I made my way from the soldiers' quarters to the labs in a hurry and found Mariella and Maki hunched over our workstation with disheveled hair and bags under their eyes.

Apparently, I hadn't been the only that had been dragged out of bed in the early hours of the morning.

"We didn't wake you, did we?" Mariella asked me, a teasing smile dancing on her lips. "I hoped at least one of us was having a restful night of sleep."

"Yeah, right," I laughed. "That's me. What do we have?"

"Just like you requested, Fen sent over the lexicon of similar languages," Maki replied. Like always, she was eager to cut the bullshit and get down to work. "I printed it out for you."

Holding a thick stack of papers, she waited until I had grabbed my seat before she pushed the documents into my hands. "I still don't know what you're trying to do, Teisha. If you're trying to look for any similarities between the Gorgos' language and—"

"It's not just that," I cut her short, holding one finger up in the air as I leafed through the lexicon, doing my best to take in as much as I could.

"I think we've been looking at this the wrong way. We're trying to extrapolate meaning out of the Gorgos' script by working on other languages because we assume it must function just like any other language. But what if it's the other way around?" I shook my head, trying to reframe my thoughts. "What if the other languages are playing by a set of rules designed by the Gorgos?"

"What are you trying to say?" Maki frowned, peering over my shoulder. I didn't reply, at least not immediately. I continued leafing through the documents in my hand until a pattern emerged, and then I placed a few of the pages down on the table.

"Look at this," I started, jabbing my finger at a couple of runes on the lexicon. "According to the Urai, this passage belongs to a race that became civilized a couple thousand years after the Gorgos. See the similarities?"

"I'm not sure I do," Mariella said, but then she narrowed her eyes as I pointed out a couple of other runes. "Are you trying to say that the Gorgos' language is a root language, like Latin was back on Earth?"

"Yeah," I smiled. "That's exactly it. The language looks so complex because we're trying to fit it backwards into patterns that evolved *from* it. Thing is, those patterns only exist because the Gorgos created them. I'd bet my hovercraft that this language right here," I continued, once more jabbing my finger at the document with all the Gorgo runes, "is the source language. A lot of the languages the Urai have compiled derive from it."

"Holy shit," Maki breathed out. She leaned back in her seat and raked one hand over her face. "I can't believe it. It's so damn obvious. You're a freaking genius, Teisha."

"Not at all," I laughed somewhat uncomfortably. I didn't feel like a genius.

I felt exhausted.

Sure, out of the three of us, I was the one with the most formal training when it came to languages, but I didn't consider myself to be as smart as Maki, and Mariella had made the original breakthrough that led us to the Urai and even the rift technology.

I was surrounded by genius and was just trying to keep up.

"It was just a hunch. I was lucky to be right."

"Yeah, right," Mariella said, rolling her eyes. "Are we playing the humble game now?"

"Seriously," I continued, "even though we're sure the Gorgos' language might be a root language, we still have a lot of work ahead of us."

"We've been at this for three straight days, barely any sleep at all between the three of us. I think we'll manage," Maki laughed, gently slapping my back in a friendly gesture.

She was right.

We had been working almost obsessively on cracking the Gorgos' script, and we showed no sign of slowing down.

As far as I was concerned, we made a great team. Sooner or later, we'd have some tangible results.

"Now, check this out," I continued, rearranging the documents in front of me. "According to what we've tallied these past few days, these three specific runes always appear in the same sequence." I leafed through the lexicon, and then laid a couple of pages next to the Gorgo alphabet. "If these other languages are anything to go by, we can surmise these three runes' meaning as—"

"Home of thought," Mariella whispered, her eyes wide. After spending so many hours trying to find a breakthrough, she could barely believe we had deciphered a small part of the puzzle. "That's what they mean. I think we can translate it as 'the mind', the place where we house our thoughts. Or 'the brain', if you want to call it that."

"What's up with all the noise?" I heard a deep voice say right behind us, and I turned in my seat to find Sa'lok strolling into the room.

He was wearing a white lab coat over his massive frame, and his muscles showed under the fabric. In his hands was a tall cup of coffee. "I was about to head to my quarters, but I heard you might be in the neighborhood. Seems like you're making progress, huh?"

"We believe we are," I said with a smile, happy to see him. Ever since this whole madness had started, and especially after the cave-in at the Puppet Master's lair, I was almost desperate to be around him. "We've managed to translate one of the most common expressions that appear in the ruins. We believe the Gorgos are referring to the brain."

"That's impressive," he nodded, taking a sip of his coffee. "The Urai couldn't do it, but the three of you together...yeah, I'm impressed."

Peering over my shoulder for a moment, he glanced at all the documents we had strewn across the table. "Oh, that's interesting. Good work on noticing it."

"Noticing what?" I frowned, having no idea what he was talking about.

"The intersection point."

"What intersection point? What are you talking about?"

"Seriously?" Cocking one eyebrow up, he placed his coffee on the table and reached for the three pictures we had of the different ruins.

"Look at the coordinates," he explained, grabbing a map and placing it under the pictures. "Do you see the way the different sites are arranged? They each come to a point at some part in their design."

"Okay…" I muttered, and then suddenly it was clear, shining as if someone had put a spotlight on it.

"Look at this!" Grabbing a pen from my breast pocket, I drew lines over the map, all of them starting on the design points of the ruins.

"Do you see it now?" I asked Maki and Mariella, their faces alive with excitement.

We all did.

The lines I'd drawn intersected.

"Holy shit," Maki muttered. "How did we miss *this*?"

"And what do we do about it?" I wondered.

SA'LOK

"This is great work," the general said, the map with the three dig sites and their intersection point in his hands.

He didn't look up from it as he spoke, his eyes still analyzing every detail. "I want you to gather a party and go see what's there. Keep it close to you and don't let it be known widely. Right now, the fewer people who know about this, the better."

"We're on it, sir," Teisha spoke up. She was standing beside me, with Maki and Mariella occupying the two chairs in front of his desk. "I've sent word to the hangar, and my hovercraft will be ready for departure in about—"

"Easy there." Putting the map away, the general finally looked up at us, his smart eyes immediately going to Teisha. There was a hint of a smile on his face. "You've all been working nonstop for the past three days, or so I've heard. I don't want you going out there exhausted. I want to do it right. Take a day or two, and then go."

"We really shouldn't wait," Teisha insisted, but the general was having none of it.

"That's an order," he said with an air of finality. "I'll defer to Sa'lok, who'll be taking point on this operation, but a day's rest is non-negotiable."

"I'll make sure of it, General," I said, trying to ignore the frown on Teisha's face.

After the breakthrough we'd had, she was more than ready to take the pilot's seat in her hovercraft. But the general had the right of it—everyone needed to rest, even if just for a night.

"That's bullshit." As we left the general's office, Teisha turned to me and crossed her arms over her chest. "There might be something important in the mountains, we know *exactly* where it might be, and the general's having us wait?"

"He's right, though," I said as patiently as I could. "You need to get some sleep."

"I'm fine," she protested. "Besides, you heard him. He said you can make the final call. So why don't we just head out there right now? We can sleep once we're back. I know Mariella and Maki are dying to get out there, as well."

Looking over Teisha's shoulder, I smiled at the two other women. Despite what Teisha was saying, the only thing that seemed to be on their minds was a warm meal and a warm bed. There were bags under their eyes, and their exhausted expressions countered Teisha's words.

"Oh, fine," she sighed, rolling her eyes. "I'll just go there myself, snap a couple of pictures from overhead, and then get back." With that, she turned on her heels and started marching down the hallway.

"You go get some rest," I told Maki and Mariella, and the two of them sighed with relief. "I'll deal with this." I took off after Teisha, and I caught up to her right before she stepped into one of the elevators that led straight down to the hangar. "Where do you think you're going?"

"I told you, I'm going to—"

"I don't think so," I laughed. Moving fast, I closed the distance between us and placed my hands on her hips.

Picking her up from the floor, I threw her over my shoulder and spun around, doubling back toward my quarters.

"Put me down," Teisha cried out, punching my back with her little fists. "What the hell, Sa'lok?"

"Orders are orders," I laughed again. "I'm just following protocol, ma'am."

"Really freaking funny." She didn't sound amused. At all.

"Thank you, ma'am," I continued, "I have always wanted to be a comedian." That just earned me a couple more punches.

I didn't really care. It felt good to be with Teisha, no one but us around.

After three days of intense work, I craved this closeness.

Once inside the bedroom, I put her down on the bed and placed my hands on my hips as I looked at her. "So, are you going to rest or will I have to tie you to the bed?"

"Is that a threat?" she smirked. "Or a promise?"

"What are you talking about?" I asked, and only then did I notice the innuendo in her voice.

Without my calling for it, adrenaline pumped through my bloodstream as I was hit with the vision of her tied beneath me, open, waiting...

"Oh, well," she shrugged, her smirk turning into a grin. "I guess I can't fight you on this, can I? If you want me to get into bed, then I'll get into bed." Still looking into my eyes, she took off her lab coat.

I wanted to turn around and give her some privacy, but my feet were glued to the floor.

I watched as she removed her tank top, her black bra hugging the perfect curve of her breasts in the most delicious way, and my body started boiling from the inside out.

Once she started swaying her hips and pushing her pants down, I realized I couldn't even blink. I swallowed hard, my cock becoming as hard as a rock.

"Is this good?" Swinging her legs off the bed, she got to her feet and took one step toward me. My eyes were drawn to hers, my heart beating at a thousand miles an hour. "Or should I take the rest off?"

In that moment, I lost it.

"More than good," I growled.

I reached for her, laying one hand on the nape of her neck and the other on her waist, and pushed her against the wall. She breathed out fast, her smile never leaving her lips, and I kissed her, ravaging her mouth, twining our tongues together as I thrust in and out, tasting her sweetness.

"I was dying for this," she gasped as I released her mouth to nip and lick my way down her throat, the need in her voice the loveliest thing I had ever heard.

"Then that makes two of us," I whispered, the hand I had on her waist traveling around the lush curves, my fingers taking in the perfect shape of her ass, pulling her tighter against me.

"Admit it." Unfastening the top of my skinsuit, she

pushed it over my shoulders, baring my chest. "You didn't bring me here because you wanted me to rest. You brought me here because you wanted *me*."

I didn't answer with words.

Instead, I just kissed her again, surrendering to the moment.

I had wanted to do this so many times, my body and mind demanding it over and over again, and now that it was happening...I couldn't even think straight.

It was a good thing I didn't have to.

All I needed to do was follow my instincts.

Taken by lust, I slid one hand up her back and unclasped her bra. I pulled back from her just so I could look at her breasts, her nipples hard with excitement, and I leaned in and took one in my mouth.

I twirled my tongue around it, feeling it hardening even more inside my mouth, and that was when Teisha reached for me.

She flattened the palm of her right hand between my legs, then wrapped her fingers around my hardness and started stroking me over my pants.

"I want you," she whispered against my lips. "I *need* you."

"I'm right here." Placing one hand between her legs, the drenched fabric of her thong against my palm, I pushed her back against the wall once more. "And I'm not going anywhere."

Dropping to my knees, I ripped the thong off her, revealing the wetness between her legs.

With a groan, I pulled her hips towards me, flicking my tongue again and again through her slick folds until she shuddered.

"Sa'lok, please," she begged, but I wasn't finished tasting her, not by a long shot.

Lifting until her legs were over my shoulders so I could bear her weight, I resumed my oral assault on her clit, sucking and licking until it throbbed in my mouth.

"I'm going to..."

With one hand gripping her hip, I slid the other forward until I could drive one, then two, fingers deep into her tight channel while I continued devouring her honey.

With a shout, she stiffened, then shook, crying her release.

With that, I spun her around and dropped her on top of the bed, the mattress shifting under her weight. As I climbed in after her, she reached for my belt and unbuckled it, her desperate fingers tugging my pants down until my erection sprung free.

Grinning, she placed her hands on my chest and forced me down until I was lying on my back.

"Right where I want you," she breathed out, climbing on top of me with cat-like movements.

Without a moment's hesitation, she grabbed my cock by the root and angled it up.

Her eyes never left mine as she pressed the tip of my hardness against her inner lips, my thickness pushing her inner walls back as I eased myself in.

"Don't hold back," she said as I rested my hands on her ass, my fingers digging into her flesh, and that was when she started rocking her hips.

Each movement of her body drove me one step closer to the edge, but she quickly realized she was right there with me. "I need you," she mumbled. "I'm—"

"I know," I cut her short, then pushed my hips up and forced her to roll to her back. I followed her and she reacted fast, lacing her legs around my waist and trapping me in place. I thrust hard and fast, driving my entire length inside her drenched pussy, then I just let it happen.

I could feel her fingernails clawing at my back, hard enough to leave marks, but I didn't care. All that mattered was the way her pussy became tighter and tighter around my hardness, her whole body shaking and twitching as she neared oblivion.

"Oh, Sa'lok," she breathed out, arching her back. "I'm gonna come."

And she did.

She moaned hard, her legs tightening around my

waist as she urged me to keep on thrusting, and I was more than happy to oblige.

I ravaged her until my body and mind were beyond ready, every single nerve ending turning into fireworks, then I just gritted my teeth and let fire and thunder explode up my spine.

"Yes, yes," she whispered against my ear as I gave her all I had, my warm seed filling her up. We didn't move for a long time. I kept my forehead pressed against hers and looked into her eyes. "This was amazing, Sa'lok."

"No," I smiled. "It was so much more than that."

By the time night came, the shadows growing long around the room, we were already fast asleep, our bodies in a tight embrace.

And even in my dreams, I knew the simple joy of it.

Sleeping by my mate.

TEISHA

" G 'morning," Sa'lok whispered as he pushed a stray lock of hair away from my face. I had one arm draped over him and my head was resting on his chest. When I opened my eyes, I found him looking down at me, a smile on his lips.

"Good morning," I repeated, narrowing my eyes as they adjusted to the light. Sunlight was filtering through the curtains, bathing the entire room in bright yellow tones.

From outside the room came the sound of hurried voices and distant laughter, a hallmark of the floor where officers like Sa'lok had their quarters. "What time is it?"

"It's almost noon," he replied, gently leaning in to

brush his lips against mine. "You slept through the entire morning. I didn't want to wake you."

"Oh, God," I groaned, pushing myself off the mattress and sitting up. "I needed a night like that. You were right. I was dead tired."

Smiling, I cupped his face with one hand and returned his kiss. More than just needing a good night's sleep, I had needed *the rest* of it.

"See? I told you."

"Yes, you did," I laughed, kicking the sheets back and jumping out of the bed. I picked up my clothes from the floor, but I took my time as I did it, fully knowing that Sa'lok's eyes were on me.

For a moment, I considered getting back into bed with him, but as much as I hated to admit it, there was something more important we needed to be doing.

"What do you say? Are we ready to hit the mountains now?"

"If you say you're ready, then I'm ready," he announced, and less than ten minutes later we were making our way toward the hangar.

On the way there, we swung by the lab and told Mariella and Maki to get ready. The two of them were already back at work, but the exhaustion I had seen on their faces last night was now gone.

"I'll be ready in thirty," Mariella chirped, hurrying out of the lab. Maki, though, didn't move. She remained standing next to her desk, her posture rigid. Her lips were a thin straight line, and she was pale.

"Is there anything wrong?" I asked her, but Sa'lok laid one hand on my shoulder and gave it a soft squeeze.

"You can stay here, if you prefer," he told her. "You'll have a consultant role on this op. Tu'ver's dying to get out of the building and do something for a change, so I might hit him up. Does that work?"

"Yes," Maki breathed out, relief washing over her face. "That'd be perfect."

As we made our way out of the lab, I threw Sa'lok a questioning glance. "What was all that about?" I asked him, not sure where Maki's hesitation had been coming from. It wasn't like we were going to war. We'd just be doing some light exploration.

"She's still reeling from what happened on the dig site she was working on," Sa'lok said. "The Gorgos attacked, they were forced into the tunnels...it was rough. Evie sent a message that Maki might need some time before she's ready to go back in the field."

"Fair enough," I nodded. Mariella would be overjoyed—Maki would be staying behind, sure, but Tu'ver would be taking her place.

The two of them were one of the first human-alien relationships that had arisen after the *Vengeance*'s crash landing, and they were going as strong as ever.

Or so the rumors said. I didn't put much stock in rumors, but the way her eyes lit up whenever we mentioned Tu'ver...yeah, Mariella was in love.

And what did that mean for me?

For us?

I... didn't know.

And now probably wasn't the time to think about it.

By the time we got to the hangar, my hovercraft had already been placed on one of the launch pads. "What the hell's that?" I cried out, hurrying toward it so I could see the fuselage up close. Someone had painted it, and the few dents in there had also been ironed out.

"I put in a work order a couple of days ago," Sa'lok smiled. "Looks good, doesn't it?"

"It looks great." I turned around to meet his gaze and returned his smile.

I wanted to go on tiptoes and kiss him right there in the middle of the hangar, but I restrained that urge.

Last night had been amazing, no doubt about it, but that didn't mean Sa'lok and I were an item.

Did it?

It was far too soon for any of that, and I sure as hell didn't want to pressure him.

Clearing my throat, I looked away from him just in time to see Mariella and Tu'ver stepping out of an elevator.

Mariella was wearing cargo pants and a light jacket

over her blouse, her boots polished to a shine. As for Tu'ver, he was wearing his tactical uniform, his vest loaded with ammo and grenades.

He looked like he was ready for war, not archeological research.

"What?" he frowned, noticing the way Sa'lok and I were staring at him. "It pays to be prepared. And after what happened at the last dig site, I can guarantee you I won't let the Gorgos catch me unprepared."

"If we're lucky, we won't come across any of those assholes," Sa'lok laughed, clasping the other K'ver's forearm.

Even though Sa'lok was an engineer by trade, most of his missions having to do with paperwork, he was still at ease among those whose sole purpose was to eliminate the enemy. That didn't surprise me.

I had seen Sa'lok in action, and as far as I was concerned, he was as good as any of the strike team leaders.

"Don't worry," Tu'ver said. "I'll cover your ass in case they show up. No need to be scared."

"Scared? I'm not the one who showed up carrying half the armory."

"If you're done fooling around, boys, I think it's time for us to go," I interrupted them, popping one of the doors open and stepping inside.

Mariella walked in after me, and I pointed her at

one of the seats in the back. Tu'ver climbed in, and the two of them settled into the seats in the vacant cargo hold. "You'll be my second," I told Sa'lok as I took my seat at the controls.

The moment I placed my hands on the yoke, I closed my eyes and took a deep breath. The last few days had been a refreshing change of pace, but nothing came close to this feeling of absolute control.

Smiling, I looked down at my dashboard and, once I was sure we were flight-ready, I started revving up the engines.

"We've been granted permission for takeoff," Sa'lok said, shouting over the mighty roar of the engines as they warmed up.

The moment I heard his words, I let some more power fly into the engines, and the hovercraft pushed itself off the pad.

Seconds later, we were cutting a straight line through Nyheim's air traffic, going up into the heights where only government aircraft had permission to go.

"We'll be there in the blink of an eye," I told everyone over the radio system, and then gave them a little taste of what I could do.

Diverting all the energy and fuel I could spare toward the engines, I turned the hovercraft into a fast-moving bullet that cut across Nyheim's blue skies.

In the distance, the jagged peaks of the mountains greeted us, wisps of clouds slowly drifting over them.

It took us close to four hours to reach the other end of the mountain range—where the intersection point was—and I started my descent once we were just a few miles from the coordinates we had.

They'd pointed toward a spot at the base of a mountain, and that's where I took us.

"What the hell's that?" I heard Mariella ask over the radio once we were close enough to see our goal clearly.

None of us had an answer. Even though nobody had really known what we'd find, I was pretty damn sure that what we were looking at hadn't been considered as an option by anyone.

Instead of the ruins we'd been expecting, or a desolate area we'd have to excavate as we had the site in the jungle, we were looking down at a massive encampment, clusters of tents merging together to make almost a city of their own.

Hundreds of tents were strewn around the base of the mountain, the barren landscape dotted with all kinds of colors.

Even from a distance, I could see people milling around down there.

Against all odds, we weren't the first ones here.

Someone had beaten us to the punch.

SA'LOK

"Please, be careful," I grumbled as Teisha lowered her hovercraft far too close to the jutting rocks for my comfort.

"Don't be such a baby." I didn't have to look at her to know she was rolling her eyes. "This isn't the first time I've done this."

"Just make sure to pick a place that's inaccessible on foot," I warned her.

"You're worried about those camps?" she asked.

"I know there's no way they didn't notice us," I said. "A low flying hovercraft tends to attract attention."

"Which is why I'm looking for ledges someone can't climb alone," she said. "However, I think it's bold of you to assume people who set up camp at the base of a mountain don't have mountain climbing equipment."

I hadn't considered that.

Teisha expertly drifted her hovercraft around the mountain so that our landing place, should we be lucky enough to find one, was out of the camp's sight.

"That could work," Mariella pointed to an outcropping.

"Look at the mountain beneath it," Teisha said. "See how it looks crumbly? That's because it is."

"I've had enough crumbling mountain sides to last me a lifetime," Tu'ver muttered.

I wasn't sure what he meant by that, but I didn't miss the smirk that appeared in the corners of Mariella's mouth.

"We could try lower on the mountain," I suggested. "It won't be as dangerous if we're not in sight of the camp."

"Good idea," Teisha nodded after some consideration. "Something is off about this mountain. I just can't put my finger on it. I'll feel better knowing we're closer to the ground."

"Never thought I'd hear those words come out of your mouth," I chuckled.

"Me, either," she agreed.

If I had to guess, I'd say we were on the exact opposite side of the mountain as the camps. Teisha finally found a rocky outcropping she was satisfied with.

It was flat enough, sturdy enough to support the weight of the hovercraft, and roughly one third up the side of the mountain.

We disembarked carefully in case the outcropping wasn't as sturdy as it looked from the air.

"We need to do recon on the camp," Tu'ver said. "No human settlements are supposed to be out here."

"Is there a law against it?" Teisha asked. "I don't want to creep around treating ordinary people like criminals."

"That's foolishly optimistic of you," I warned her. "Remember the world we're living in now. We have to assume a group of humans purposefully separating themselves from society in secret are up to something unsavory."

"I know you're right," she sighed. "Just let me pretend the world isn't as horrible as it is for a moment, okay?"

"Okay," I nodded. "You go ahead and spin your fantasies while I prep the climbing equipment."

"Deal."

I made my way to the storage compartment under the hovercraft and pulled out crates of rope, grappling hooks, attachable cleats, and anything else we might need.

Tu'ver appeared beside me.

"Why do you do that?" he asked.

"Do what?"

"Indulge her delusion," he said.

"She's not deluded," I replied. "She knows full well why we have to check out the camps. I just don't like completely crushing the optimism out of her. Not too many people have it anymore."

"Optimism doesn't serve people in times like these," Tu'ver said solemnly.

"I disagree. I think it helps the humans cling to their humanity," I replied.

"As long as she doesn't get in the way," he replied.

"That's a fine way to talk about the woman who just flew us here. Mariella would be disappointed in you."

That seemed to shut him up.

"You're right," he nodded. "It's difficult knowing we've likely found another host farm."

"Is that what we're calling them now?"

"Can you think of a better name for a place set up by the Gorgos to collect human host bodies?" he asked.

"No, but that doesn't mean I like calling it a host farm."

"None of us do," he replied.

"We can tie off the ropes here," Teisha called suddenly.

Tu'ver and I turned our attention to her. She stood by a thick outcrop of stone fused into the side of the mountain.

"Told you she's not deluded," I murmured to Tu'ver.

"She could still be deluded," he muttered back. "But at least she's helpful."

"I'm going to tell Mariella you think a sunny outlook is delusional," I taunted.

"You don't have to," Mariella's voice came from behind me. "I've been standing over here the whole time."

She pointed to an area concealed behind the body of the hovercraft.

"Good," I grinned. "Please tell your mate that there's nothing wrong with looking on the bright side."

Mariella barked out a laugh.

"Don't you think I've been trying that since I met him?" she grinned. "He's a right old stick in the mud, but I love him anyway."

"Thank you, darling," Tu'ver smiled. "I love you, too, despite your deliriously happy outlook on life."

"So long as it keeps me sane," she shrugged.

I couldn't help but feel a small pang of jealousy for what Tu'ver and Mariella had.

If their characteristics and attributes were written out side by side, they wouldn't appear to be compatible.

Yet here they were. It must be nice to have that kind of unconditional love, the kind found only in a mate.

For a moment as I'd drifted off to sleep last night, I'd felt something like it.

Or maybe I was the delusional one.

I shook the thoughts away. I had a job to do and I needed to focus on it.

I brought the ropes to Teisha and she secured them around the rock.

"Can you tighten them?" she asked. "I think they're probably tight enough, but I'd feel much better knowing those burly arms of yours gave the ends a tug."

I pulled on the ropes until the knots were so tightly wound together, I knew we'd have to cut the ropes loose if we ever wanted to use them again.

Teisha looked everything over once more and nodded with satisfaction.

Harnesses and hooks were distributed. Soon, all four of us were over the edge of the outcropping, skirting around the side of the mountain to overlook the camp.

We didn't speak to each other during the climb.

As we neared the camp, we moved with more caution. If anyone in the camp spotted us, we wouldn't be able to escape easily.

"Look over there," Mariella whisper-shouted. She jerked her chin in the direction of the camp. I turned to see what she was looking at. She'd spotted a cluster of rocks, each bigger than I was, that would make a good perch.

I reached out and tapped Teisha's shoulder,

indicating that she should make her way over to that spot. The others followed.

Soon, we were all concealed behind the boulders.

"Any signs of Gorgo infections?" I asked.

"Nothing," Tu'ver answered. "Even with my vision at max, all of their eyes are clear. They're moving and socializing normally."

"Maybe we really did stumble upon an independent colony," Teisha said wistfully.

"We should be so lucky," Mariella sighed in agreement. "It's so tiring stumbling upon threat after threat after threat."

"I think I know who they are," Tu'ver said, his tone dark.

"Who?" I demanded.

"I think we've found the new anti-alien headquarters," Tu'ver muttered.

"For fuck's sake," Teisha muttered. "What are they doing out here? You don't think it's another attempt to start an alien-free civilization, do you?"

"I can't say for sure," Tu'ver replied. "But I can see they have weapons. General Rouhr needs to know about this. It looks like they're planning something big. It can't be a coincidence that they're here."

"Not after our last run-in with those weirdos," Teisha muttered. "They're too happy to deal with the Gorgos."

"I'll call it in," I said.

Pulling back from the rocks, I hunkered over my comms unit. "That telepathic connection with the Puppet Master would have been useful about now," I grumbled.

But underneath, I was still worried. What had the Gorgoxians done to our ally?

Would he ever return?

And if he didn't, did that mean Ankau itself was in danger?

A soft chime let me know my comm had finally been patched through.

"Are you there already?" the general asked. "I didn't expect a report for another hour."

"Have you seen how Teisha flies?" I asked. "But it's for the best. We have a situation here."

After a brief report, General Rouhr informed me he'd gather additional information about the camp.

"Stay low, but keep looking for anything unusual," he ordered.

"That would be everything," I muttered, but well after he'd signed off.

"Now what?" Teisha looked at me.

"There's not much the four of us can do about the camp," I said. "We're hilariously outnumbered. It's best to stay out of sight until we hear from General Rouhr again."

"In that case, I say we get to work on what we came here to do," she said.

"Let's go back to the other side of the mountain," Tu'ver suggested. "We can explore from there without risking detection."

"Does that mean more grappling?" Mariella sighed.

"Yes, dearest," Tu'ver answered. "If you'd like, you can attach your harness to mine and cling onto my back."

"I'd like that, thanks," Mariella grinned.

"Do you need to ride on my back?" Teisha asked me with a smirk.

"No, but I was going to offer to toss you up the mountain if you prefer?"

"That works for me."

We laughed as we prepared our equipment for the climb back.

We were about halfway between the camp and the hovercraft when Mariella pointed to something a few yards above us.

"Does that look natural to you?" she asked Teisha, who had to crane her neck to see what Mariella was talking about. Teisha happened to be positioned directly above me on the mountain, blocking my view.

"No, it doesn't," she answered.

"Care to clue me in?" I asked.

"There's an opening in the side of the mountain. It looks carved," she called down. "I say we climb up."

"I'll follow you," I confirmed.

After a taxing vertical climb, the four of us stood on a narrow ledge hardly big enough to fit all of us.

The opening in question looked like a clumsy archway. It was impossible to tell from here how far it extended into the mountain.

Teisha pulled out a flashlight and shone it into the darkness. The light reflected in the eyes of a few cave-dwelling critters, but nothing looked concerning.

"I'm game if you are," she said to me.

"Lead the way."

TEISHA

My bravado might have fooled the others, but not Sa'lok. He must've known I was trying to put on a brave face, but he didn't say anything when I ducked into the dark, cramped space.

I hadn't thought getting caught in that cave-in in the desert messed me up, but apparently, it had.

The idea of going into the mountain made me feel sick to my stomach. No matter how many times I told myself I wasn't underground, my body and subconscious wouldn't listen to me.

Going into the mountain like this *felt* like being underground and that was all that mattered.

"Are you sure you're alright?" Sa'lok asked me in a casual tone.

"Not at all," I replied lightly.

"We can turn back," he offered.

"No way!" I protested. "This is obviously something relevant to what we're looking for. We can't turn back."

"It might not be what we're looking for," he suggested.

"Are you kidding?" I barked out a laugh. "We find a man-made tunnel bored into the side of the mountain and you want to tell me it might not be what we're looking for?"

"I know it's what we're looking for," he smirked. "I'm just trying to make you feel better. Is it working?"

I paused. My breath wasn't coming as rapidly as it had been a moment ago.

"Yes, it is." I declared.

"Good, then I'll keep pissing you off until the anxiety ebbs away completely."

"You're such a good friend."

"I know," he beamed.

His reaction to the word 'friend' gave me pause. Surely, we were more than friends now, weren't we? It was still something we needed to talk about.

I knew now wasn't the time, but was there ever a good time for a talk like that?

The more I thought about it, the more anxious I was.

Somehow, sorting out my relationship with Sa'lok

in official terms was more anxiety-inducing than the notion of being trapped beneath rocks again.

What the hell was wrong with me?

Somewhere above us, a few pebbles came loose from the side of the mountain. The skittering sound that echoed through the tunnel made my heart start racing all over again. I stopped dead in my tracks.

I didn't want to stop, really.

My panicked shit-heel of a subconscious gave me no choice in the matter.

Sa'lok gently took my hand and led me forward.

"The tunnel is perfectly sound," he assured me. "We're still low in the mountain. A little hole in the base won't bring the whole thing down."

I could've pointed out that the path we were on was slowly inclining, but I didn't.

Instead, I decided to take comfort in his words and the steady feeling of my hand in his.

"You mentioned that this was man-made a moment ago," Mariella spoke up. "I'm not sure that's accurate."

"You think this is natural?" Sa'lok asked.

"Not at all. I just don't think humans did it," she corrected. "Teisha, look at the walls. Can you think of any human tools that could do this?"

"Do what?"

I shone my light on the wall. At first, I didn't see anything, then I realized that was the point. I didn't see *anything.* No tool marks, no tracks in the stone. Nothing to indicate any human terraforming tools I was familiar with.

The stone wasn't perfectly smooth, either. Water erosion hadn't made these tunnels. It was as if someone, or something, had taken a very powerful laser and crudely drawn an archway.

"I see your point," I said to Mariella. "Humans had nothing to do with this, but someone else sure as hell did."

"Don't look at us," Tu'ver shrugged. "I can't think of anything we possess that could make these tunnels."

"And I can't think of a reason why any of us would want to make a secret mountain tunnel," Sa'lok added.

"Wait, Tu'ver!" Mariella called sharply. Tu'ver froze. "What?"

"Swing your headlamp back the other way!"

Tu'ver looked to his right. Mariella sighed.

"Your *other* other way," she corrected.

Tu'ver looked directly at the wall. His headlamp illuminated hundreds of lines of impossibly tiny markings.

"Isn't that the same language from the other sites?" I asked.

"I think it is." Mariella was practically shaking with excitement. "Hurry, let's document this."

"Right, because the etchings in stone might not be

around for much longer," Sa'lok teased.

"We didn't bring anything to assist translation, did we?" Mariella asked me.

"Everything is still in the hovercraft," I replied.

"Damn," she muttered. "At least I have a camera, not that it'll help us now."

She pulled out a small black device and captured a few images.

"Maki and Alyssa will be excited to see those pictures," I offered.

"That's a nice thought," Tu'ver said. "An even nicer thought would be knowing what we're walking into."

"Did you skip breakfast today?" Mariella gave him a hard look. "You're uncharacteristically grumpy."

"Is he?" Sa'lok chuckled. "This is how he is normally."

"He's right," Tu'ver nodded. "I'm only nice to you." He pressed a kiss into Mariella's cheek, making her giggle.

I glanced at Sa'lok from the corner of my eye. He smiled at me. I was glad for the darkness. It hid the blush creeping up my cheeks.

I don't know what had gotten into me. The best thing about Sa'lok was that I could tell him anything.

Somehow, though, I couldn't make myself say that I adored him and wanted to be with him. The risk seemed far too great. How could I want something that could put our friendship at risk? Didn't that make me a bad friend?

I supposed I became a bad friend the moment I decided to hop into bed with him, not that I regretted it. I needed to stop getting all up in my own head about this.

Sa'lok and I were uncomplicated.

We'd always been that way. Why shouldn't I just go back to being uncomplicated about things?

That sounded like less of a headache for me.

"What are you thinking about?" Sa'lok asked suddenly.

"What?" I jumped a little at the sound of his voice.

"You've got this fierce look on your face," he said. "I figured you were thinking hard about something and I felt that I should disturb you."

I laughed.

See? Sa'lok was being uncomplicated and fun, as usual. I should be able to do the same.

"I was thinking about the writing on the wall," I said. "And that I enjoy holding your hand."

"The idea of holding my hand made you make that face? I know how your face looks when you're enjoying something and that was not that face."

"I swear I enjoy holding your hand," I protest. "It's just that I wasn't sure if it was weird to enjoy holding your hand."

"That's the stupidest thing you've ever said," Sa'lok laughed. "And I've seen you do some pretty stupid things, so keep that in mind."

"So, you don't feel weird?" I asked.

"No," he shook his head. "I don't feel weird about enjoying holding your hand. I don't feel weird that I want to drag you into my bed the moment I have a bed to drag you into. Does that make you feel weird?"

"Yes, but only because we're having this discussion in a public forum." I jerked my head in the direction of Mariella and Tu'ver, who were looking at us with equal parts dismay and amusement.

"Fair point. We can pick this discussion up later," he grinned.

At that moment, both his and Tu'ver's comms units lit up like a fireworks display.

"That looks important," I said.

Sa'lok and Tu'ver grabbed their units and opened the communications channels.

"I can't believe we get signal in here," Mariella mused.

"Our augmented tech is a natural signal booster," Sa'lok explained, spreading his hand to show how brightly his circuits glowed. Without thinking, I reached out and traced my finger across his skinsuit.

He smiled at my touch.

"General Rouhr wants us back outside," Tu'ver said.

"He's mobilized the strike teams. He needs us to navigate them to the camps."

"The anti-alien campers aren't going to like that," I tutted.

"I know," Sa'lok said. "You and Mariella should stay here, away from the conflict."

"No way!" I protested.

"Think about it," Sa'lok urged. "You don't have any weapons. You're not trained to use any of mine, even if I had spares. You and Mariella are far more useful here, where you have a better chance of figuring out the significance of the mountain. You handle this, we handle the camp, and we save time in the process."

I wanted to argue, but I couldn't.

"Damn your logic," I muttered. "You're right. Go fight your battles. Mariella and I will keep working."

"That's my lady." Sa'lok stroked my cheek and I nearly melted into a puddle on the floor.

Before I could second guess myself, I grabbed his shirt and pulled him in for a kiss. His lips pressed against mine. Our mouths fit together perfectly.

"We haven't got all day," Tu'ver called, already halfway back to the opening in the side of the mountain.

"See you soon," Sa'lok winked. I watched him walk away until the darkness swallowed him up.

SA'LOK

"There's something strange about this mountain," Tu'ver muttered as we carefully slid down the mountain face. It was a delicate balance of moving swiftly while avoiding drawing unwanted attention from the camp.

Not tumbling down the mountain ass over face was also a priority as far as I was concerned.

"There are a lot of strange things about this mountain," I replied. "Take your pick."

"Have you noticed all the outcroppings?" he asked.

"Sure," I shrugged, not understanding his point.

"I get the sense that they aren't the product of erosion or landslides," he continued. "They're too conveniently placed."

"I don't know about that." I was only half listening.

Most of my concentration went toward keeping both feet on the mountainside.

"Oh, really?" Tu'ver challenged. "Take a look."

He pointed straight up the side of the mountain. Once I secured my footing, I looked up, as well. From below, the outcroppings didn't look random at all. In fact, they reminded me of balconies for apartments, though not evenly distributed.

"I see what you mean," I said.

"I wonder if this mountain was a place of residence," he continued. "The temple Amira and Dax explored showed no signs of anyone living there, but this mountain feels different."

"The women are still exploring," I reminded him. "Perhaps they'll have discovered something when we rejoin them."

"Hopefully that'll be sooner rather than later," Tu'ver grunted as he hauled himself over a sizable slab of rock. I followed suit.

Together, we lay on our bellies and pulled ourselves to the edge of another outcropping.

"You're right," I nodded. "These flat outcroppings are incredibly convenient. I wonder if the past residents were into sunbathing."

"Don't let your circuits overheat," Tu'ver warned me.

He took out his sniper rifle, peered through the scope, and grunted with distaste.

"What?" I asked.

"They're better armed than I originally realized," he said. "I assumed they'd salvaged whatever weapons they could from fallen soldiers or stole from human armories."

"They didn't?"

"From the looks of it, someone in that camp has access to custom weapons and plenty of them. The tech isn't entirely human, either."

"What are you suggesting?" I asked.

"Either the anti-alien groups have found another temple to raid or they have a beneficiary."

Skrell.

I immediately thought of the madwoman Teisha and I had faced in the Puppet Master's cavern.

Maybe her little group wasn't the exception to the rule anymore.

"We assumed a human host farm was out here," I recalled. "Perhaps the Gorgos are involved in the sudden appearance of an encampment that, somehow, managed to escape our detection."

"My thoughts exactly."

"What if somehow they're passing technical knowledge to their hosts?"

"Aren't you a ray of sunshine," he grumbled.

Before I could dwell on the possibility for too long, the strike team aerial units appeared over the tree line. To no one's surprise, the camp's sentry sounded the alarm. Within seconds, a thunderous blast echoed off the mountainside.

"Was that what I think it was?" I asked.

"A cannon? Yes, it was," Tu'ver confirmed. "I don't know how they got such heavy weapons out here."

I grabbed my comms unit and signaled the strike team leaders.

"All units be advised," I spoke briskly into the mouthpiece. "The camp is heavily armed. Expect anti-aircraft weaponry. Details on weapons and ammunition currently unknown."

Each unit acknowledged my message. I wished I could give them more information. Unfortunately, I'd only heard the weapon. I hadn't seen it or what it launched.

"Looks like the strike teams are landing," Tu'ver pointed out.

What?

Why?

Sure enough, the aerial units were settling down somewhere within the forest.

I fumbled for my comms unit.

"Status report," I demanded, even though I didn't have the authority to demand anything.

"They're forcing us to go in on foot," someone replied. It might've been Karzin or Sk'lar. Everyone sounded the same on the comms unit. "The anti-aircraft cannons are set up in too tight of a pattern. They've got someone at the trigger with a sharp eye. If we come in for a strafing run, chances are too high they'll take us out instead."

My fist tightened on the comm. "It's not a good choice at all."

"It's the best one we have right now."

"What's the plan of attack?" I hoped there was something brilliant planned.

"Attack," someone else said.

"You've got to be kidding me!" I snapped.

"We're coming in with hardly any briefing." I was certain that was Vrehx's voice.

Only he was able to sound bored and annoyed at the same time. "We have to play to our strengths and this is the least bad of all the options. Everyone out here does pretty well at hand-to-hand. And it's not like we're facing the Xathi."

"Skrell," I hissed.

"Language, soldier," Vrehx snapped, but I was no longer listening.

"I have to get down there," I said. "They're outnumbered."

"Go," Tu'ver urged. "I'll watch your back." He patted his sniper rifle as if it were a beloved pet.

"Don't shoot me by mistake," I muttered as I launched myself out of our rocky cover.

"If I shoot you, it won't be a mistake," Tu'ver called after me.

If that was his idea of encouragement, he needed to attend a seminar or something.

Luckily, most of the enemy fighters were paying attention to the hoard of aliens running their way.

I was able to drop into the camp unnoticed, except for two camp residents. All I had to do was knock their heads together to silence them.

Before I dove headfirst into the fray, I looked back up the side of the mountain for Tu'ver. I couldn't see him.

Good.

"I'll slit your fucking throat!" A screeching howl tore my attention from the mountain. I'd been spotted. A well-armed rabble-rouser had discovered me and the two unconscious men at my feet.

He must've assumed they were dead, which they weren't. At least, not to my knowledge. I hadn't smacked their skulls together that hard.

"You don't have to do this," I warned my attacker. It was a courtesy at that point. I always liked to give my opponents a chance to opt out. It felt more honorable when I took their lives.

I always resorted to killing only as a last resort, however this wasn't the first time I'd tangled with a fanatic. The last resort always seemed to be the only option when it came to them. Shame.

"I won't stop until you're all dead at my feet," my attacker hissed.

"I'm sorry you feel that way."

I unsheathed my knife. Not surprisingly, my attacker laughed. He raised his blaster, pointing it right between my eyes. I wasn't worried. His hand was shaking. He'd either had too many stimulant pills or not enough to eat. I'd guess it was the former.

A twitchy trigger finger wasn't ideal for me, but his reflexes would be dulled.

I ducked and made a mad dash for his legs. As I'd expected, he fired his blaster half a second too late, missing me completely.

He braced himself, preparing to be tackled at the knees, but I changed tactics. I whirled around, coming up behind him.

I'd been waiting for a chance to use my knife. The knife itself wasn't anything special. It was forged in the armory with basic techniques and simple metals. It was what coated the blade that made it special.

The tonic I'd concocted was meant to cause the sensation of pins and needles throughout the entire body. It made it difficult to stand, grip things, and the like, but it wasn't as dangerous as a paralysis serum.

I lifted the blade, ready to observe rather than fight. I was a scientist at heart, after all.

Before I could lift the blade to my attacker's neck, his head exploded.

"What the skrell?" I hissed and released the now headless body. Surely, my chemical tonic couldn't do that? I hadn't even touched him yet.

A quick examination of what was left of the skull told me the death shot hadn't come from the direction of the camp behind me, but the mountain in front of me.

Tu'ver was a damn good shot.

I whipped out my comms unit.

"You didn't have to ruin my field test," I said to him.

"Sorry, you were taking too long and I got bored."

"I have half a mind to use you as a test subject," I snapped.

"Go ahead and try," he chuckled. "You'll be dead before you take the first step."

I'd forgotten the dark humor of combat. It was always better to laugh than to lose yourself to anger.

The fight in the center of the camp had escalated into something fierce. I took my time selecting when and how I'd jump in.

I had a unique vantage point. Most of the fanatics

still had their backs to me. They believed the threat came only from the front gates of the camp.

I snuck up behind one and jabbed him with the tip of my knife.

"What the fuck?" he snarled, whirling around. Already his muscles were behaving clumsily.

"What did you do to me, scum?" he demanded.

"I believe you humans use the term 'fallen asleep'," I explained. "I've made all of your limbs fall asleep."

"What?" he muttered, on his knees, looking confused.

"If you start crawling, you might be able to find shelter before the pins and needles make bearing weight impossible," I advised as I stepped over him. He took a sloppy swing at me and missed entirely.

"I like this serum," I said to myself, flipping the blade.

I continued slipping into battle to puncture opponents. I figured I could be most useful by helping strike team members overwhelmed with more than two opponents. Every so often, I'd see one of the enemy seize up and fall to the ground for no reason. I knew it was Tu'ver's handiwork.

The more I watched the fanatics, the more I noticed the oddness in their movements. It wasn't drastic or consistent, but it was there. Sometimes, a normally clumsy fighter would briefly be blessed with speed and strength to rival a Valorni, only to return to the clumsy state once more.

It had to be Gorgo interference. It wasn't the full takeover we'd seen before. The fanatics weren't rabid and uncontrollable, well, not more than usual.

I suspected the Gorgos were influencing the fanatics to be better fighters.

How? I wasn't sure.

Was it like technical knowledge that they could pass on, or something else?

Something more dangerous?

I knew in my bones that it had something to do with the mountain. Whatever was inside it was worth protecting.

TEISHA

We'd been walking forever.

Alright. Probably not actually forever.

But between my stress at being underground, and worry over Sa'lok, it seemed like it.

"Fen took a look at the pictures from earlier," Mariella declared.

"Can she tell us anything?"

Mariella frowned at her comms unit.

"Unfortunately, no," she sighed. "But she hasn't had them for long. She's going to keep trying."

"I'm sorry I couldn't be of more help."

"What?" Mariella laughs. "You've been more than enough help. We wouldn't have gotten here if it wasn't for you. Hell, we wouldn't have figured out we needed to come here if it wasn't for you."

"I'm a linguist who failed at deciphering a language," I pointed out. "That's sort of my one job."

"I don't think that applies to previously unknown alien languages," Mariella said. "It'll likely be a few years before we have a working idea of what this language is. We're dealing with less than the bare minimum and look at all we've accomplished."

"Do you practice these kinds of pep talks in the mirror or are you just naturally good at them?" I smile.

"It comes naturally," she grinned. "Leena often got discouraged as a child. She'd come up with these crazy experiments, then get upset when they didn't work with twigs, leaves, mud, and whatever else we had in our backyard. I had to get pretty good at pep talks to avoid full-scale meltdowns. Have you met my sister?"

"Briefly," I nodded. "She seems brilliant, though intense."

"That's exactly right," Mariella laughed. "Believe it or not, she's become less intense over the years."

"What's her secret?" I asked.

"Steady work and good sex."

I nearly choked on my inhale.

"Is that why you're so mild-mannered?" I asked.

Mariella tipped her head back and laughed.

"No, but it sure helps! Why are you blushing so much? Aren't you and Sa'lok together?"

"We might be," I said after a moment of thought.

"What do you mean?" Mariella tilted her head to one side. "You both seem so close and so settled."

"We've been friends for an age," I replied.

"I was getting a distinct more-than-friends vibe," she said.

"We've ventured beyond friend territory lately," I admitted.

"That's great!" she beamed.

"Is it? What if it doesn't work? It's impossible to go back to being friends."

"Is it?"

"Isn't it?"

"I don't think so," she shrugged. "Sure, it might be awkward, but I believe anyone can get past awkwardness and strange feelings if the friendship means enough to them."

"I suppose you're right," I considered. "I haven't thought about it that way."

"It's none of my business," she started, "but it sounds to me like you're assuming everything is going to go wrong."

"Sa'lok did suggest I cut back on my optimism," I joked.

"He defended your optimism to Tu'ver before we climbed down to the camp."

"He did?"

Mariella nodded.

"So, why do you assume things won't work out between you two?" she asked.

"I don't know," I shrugged. I didn't want to think about this, not right now. I wanted to think about it later when I wasn't walking deeper into the heart of a mountain with every step. "I suppose it's a good idea to hope for the best but expect the worst."

"I hear a lot of people say that," she said thoughtfully. "Personally, I think it's a load of crap."

"Oh, do you?"

"I do," she nodded. "There's nothing wrong with hoping with your whole heart that things will go the way you want them to. What's the worst that can happen?"

Was this a trick question?

"Things don't go the way you want them to," I reply.

"Right. And will that kill you?"

"I mean, if you're hoping the bullet doesn't strike your heart and it does, it's going to kill you."

"And is Sa'lok a bullet?"

"You know, I've heard rumors that Leena is the scary sister but, from where I'm standing, you're much scarier."

"Don't dodge the question."

"No, losing Sa'lok wouldn't kill me. He's not a bullet. But losing his friendship would be pretty damn painful."

"So, correct me if I'm wrong, but you'd rather only put a portion of your hope and efforts into having something amazing with him instead of putting your whole heart into it and risking losing him?"

"I didn't say that," I blurted.

"Your body language did. Answer the question."

"Yes, I guess."

"Don't you think only putting a portion of your effort in will guarantee failure? Don't you think things will work out the way you want them to if you put your whole heart into it?"

"You're giving me a headache," I muttered.

"And you're still avoiding the question," Mariella pointed out. "He's crazy about you. You're crazy about him. The chemistry between you both is insane. What's the problem?"

"There's no problem," I said. "I want him more than I've ever wanted anything."

"And he wants you, too."

"I'd like to hear that from him before I take any leaps of faith."

It felt weird making such a personal confession to anyone but Sa'lok.

"We can talk about something else if you want?" Mariella asked.

"Actually, yeah. That'd be nice," I nodded. "You've given me a lot to mull over."

"No, I didn't," she smiled. "You were already thinking about all those things long before I said them out loud."

"You're right," I admitted with a laugh.

We walked through the tunnel. It suddenly curved until I was sure we'd doubled back on ourselves. Light from up ahead illuminated the walls and floor.

"What an odd path," Mariella marveled.

"I wonder where we are," I murmured.

Mariella and I stepped into the light. I blinked rapidly, willing my eyes to adjust more quickly. When they did, I realized we were on a ledge not unlike the one in front of the first entrance to the tunnel. This one was wider and hugged the mountain until it reached another, identical opening.

"It's like a balcony of sorts," Mariella commented. "Do you think it had a purpose or was purely for aesthetics?"

"Your guess is as good as mine."

Below us, the anti-alien encampment swarmed with activity. General Rouhr's strike teams had arrived. I didn't know much about battle tactics, but I could tell it wasn't going well. The general's soldiers didn't have the numbers, even if they did have more brawn and superior weapons. They couldn't go on like that indefinitely.

"Do you think they've called for reinforcements?" I asked.

"Doubtful," Mariella shook her head. "General Rouhr said he mobilized the strike teams. Everyone who could act as reinforcement is from a ground team. They'd have to report in at Nyheim and take off from there. It would take at least an hour, even if they were already close to Nyheim."

"There aren't any ground teams posted nearby?"

"No," she replied. "No one is supposed to be out here."

"No wonder those asshole groups picked this place."

"I'm not sure that's the only reason."

"How do you mean?" I took my eyes off the battle below to look at Mariella.

"We can discuss theories later, but too much is happening around this mountain for it all to be unrelated."

Tu'ver had said something similar before. I was inclined to agree. But Mariella was right. We could theorize when this was over.

"We've got to do something," I insisted.

"Like what?" Mariella asked. "It's not like we can go charging down there. We'd be shot down before we even cleared the mountain."

"I know," I groaned, feeling frustrated. "How long do you think it would take us to get back to my hovercraft?

It's got a small defense blaster. If anything, it would cause a distraction."

"Too long," she sighed. "We've spent well over two hours in these tunnels and that's just my best guess."

"Two hours walking. What if we sprinted?"

"We'd still have the climbing portion. We can't speed that up."

"I can't handle this." I brought my hands up to my hair. "I can't stand not being down there helping Sa'lok."

"He's a talented fighter," Mariella assured me. "And I'm sure Tu'ver's keeping an eye out for him."

"Tu'ver's probably busy fighting," I pointed out. Mariella fixed me with a mischievous smirk.

"You don't know much about Tu'ver, do you?"

"We've only just met," I reminded her.

"He's a master sniper," she told me. "He's the best on the team. I guarantee you he's found a perfect perch and is keeping those fanatics off Sa'lok's back."

"That makes me feel better," I sighed. "But I still don't feel right about being up here, doing nothing."

I glanced at Mariella, but she wasn't looking at me. She was looking behind us, at the mountain. When she turned back to face me, she smiled.

"I might have a plan."

"Care to share?"

"See that boulder over there?" She pointed to a huge

rock that was almost the same size as my hovercraft. It was precariously perched not far from where the rock ledge we stood on ended.

"What about it?"

"Look where it'll end up if it happens to fall."

I followed the imaginary track the boulder would make. It would land smack on top of the camp, crushing at least one hastily built structure in the process.

"Do you think that would work?" I asked her.

"I know it will," she beamed. "I've done it before."

"That's deeply comforting and deeply concerning at the same time."

"Just trust me on this."

I hesitated before answering.

"Why not?" I shrugged. "It's better than sitting here twiddling our thumbs."

"Exactly. Now, help me get over this ridge."

SA'LOK

This wasn't going well, at all.

No matter what we did, the bastards kept coming. The serum I'd dipped my blade in wore off long ago. I hadn't brought any extra.

My best chance of being useful was to take cover and fire my handheld blaster.

My ammunition was coated with another serum of my own invention. This one dulled all of the senses and created a perpetual sensation of vertigo. As much as I wanted to, I had no time to marvel at the serum's effectiveness.

We'd expected a rabble, a mob.

More fanatics, like the ones we'd tangled with before.

We were wrong.

At this point, it was safe to call them an army. They were trained. They were armed. The Gorgos were boosting their abilities, albeit temporarily and only one man at a time.

We were in over our heads. That didn't happen often. I wasn't sure what to do.

No, that wasn't true. I knew what to do.

I would give everything I had to take as many of these assholes as I could down with me. Each one that fell to my blaster or my blade was one less alive to harm Teisha.

Skrell, I'd really mucked things up with her, hadn't I?

I should've told her exactly how I felt the moment I knew I loved her. It hadn't taken long. If I was being honest with myself, I'd loved her from the moment I first saw her.

That was back when she was first assigned to run supply missions during the final days of the war against the Xathi.

I thought I was doing her, myself, and everyone around us a favor by developing a friendship with her and not letting it go any further.

I didn't want to be a distraction or to be distracted while we had the Xathi to deal with.

I figured once the Xathi were handled, I'd have a

chance to talk to her about being more than friends, but that chance never came.

There was the confusion with the Puppet Master, rebuilding the human settlements, and now the Gorgos.

I'd been a fool to think I could set my feelings for her to the side.

There would never be a perfect time, just time we could have been together.

"Look what we have here," a sneer tore me from my thoughts. My hiding spot had been found. It was bound to happen eventually.

"Look at the slimy scum," another sneer followed the first.

Five fanatics surrounded me, cutting off my escape. I fired my blaster at one of them. Nothing happened. I was out of ammunition.

Skrell.

I tore my blade from its sheath. The fanatics laughed in my face.

"Remember when we used to think the aliens were scary?" one chuckled.

I'd been crouching behind some storage crates for the sake of maximizing the element of surprise. Now that I'd been discovered, there was no reason to stay low. I stretched up to my full height. I towered over even the tallest of the fanatics.

Not going to lie, seeing their faces blanch was satisfying.

At my best, I could handle three of them in hand-to-hand combat. Not five. Even if they hadn't figured it out yet, I knew this wouldn't end favorably for me.

"Come on," I snarled. "Who's brave enough to make the first move!"

Even knowing that they outnumbered and outgunned me, they hesitated.

"Suit yourselves," I grinned and flipped my blade.

They scattered when I darted forward. I caught one of them in the arm with my blade, though without the serum it was little more than a paper cut.

"Son of a bitch," he snarled, whirling around to strike me in the chest. I didn't flinch, but he sure did.

He'd struck my circuits, which was akin to punching a control panel. Thankfully, my augmented tech was sturdier than the average control panel.

I smashed my fist into the side of his head, dazing him. By now, the others realized that they couldn't just stand there. I knew they'd figure it out sooner or later. I'd been hoping for later.

The one I'd just struck in the head crumpled to the ground. He wasn't knocked out, just dazed. He'd be back on his feet swinging at me again sooner than I would've liked.

One of the fanatics charged me. I blocked him, but

quickly realized he was nothing but a distraction so someone else could drive armored knuckles into my side. My ribs didn't appreciate the assault.

I brought my knee up, driving it into the groin of the man who'd charged me. A low blow, but I couldn't make myself feel bad.

Suddenly, my comm started squawking. "Heads up, guys!"

Mariella?

She continued for a few seconds, but I couldn't focus on what she was saying.

Something about rocks? Maybe they'd found more writing.

It would have to wait.

As I fought the five fanatics, I saw glimpses of the fight happening in the center of the camp. Every strike team member I saw was in a similar situation as me. Too many fanatics and not enough weapons.

This wasn't going to end well.

I hoped Teisha was safely inside the mountain, unaware of how badly things were going down here.

I didn't hear the rumbling at first. It blended in with the usual din of battle. It was only when it escalated into something like a roar that I paused. The fanatics paused, as well. They heard it, too.

"Shit!" one swore, and immediately ran away. The

others quickly followed suit, looking over their shoulders at the looming mountain as they ran.

I looked up the mountain as well.

My jaw dropped.

Rocks.

An avalanche of stones tumbled down the mountain, doubling in speed with every passing second. At the forefront of the rockslide was a boulder large enough to take out an aerial unit.

The fanatics had a good idea for once. I spun around and ran as fast as I could.

"Rockslide," I shouted as I ran through the fight. "Take cover!"

How did one take cover from a gigantic, speeding boulder?

I grabbed as many of the strike team members as I could and urged them to get out of the enclosed camp. The only downside was, the entrance to the camp was directly in the path of the rockslide.

The first boulder slammed into one of the camp's storage buildings.

As I ran, a fanatic made a half-assed attempt to trip me. I stumbled, grabbing onto his sleeve for balance. He tripped and fell. I didn't.

I didn't look behind me to see if the rockslide had eaten him up. His screams told me the answer.

As soon as I cleared the camp, I veered off toward the tree line.

The border of the camp was enough to stop most of the rockslide. Some mid-sized boulders and slabs were launched over the border and into the tree line, but those were easy to keep clear of.

When the dust settled, the camp was in bad shape. Fanatics stumbled out of their ruined camp, bleeding and bruised.

I wagered we'd destroyed most, if not all, of their supplies and shelter. Hundreds of them gathered beyond the camp fence. They glared at us, their eyes glinting under a thick coating of dust and grime.

I braced myself for the fight to continue. Now that most of them had sustained injuries and lacked weapons, I felt less dire about our odds. The fanatics knew that, as well. They didn't resume the fight.

My comms unit hissed to life. Someone's garbled voice came through. I couldn't make out anything. I shook the unit and tapped the sides, dislodging dust and small pebbles that had gotten caught in its tiny crevasses.

"Oh, skrell, that was good!" came a cheerful, crackling voice.

"Tu'ver?" I blurted. "Is that you?"

"Damn right!" he whooped. I'd never heard him sound so excited.

"You didn't have something to do with that rockslide, did you?"

"No, but I know who did." I could practically hear him grinning through the commlink.

"Oh?"

"Mariella!"

"You're joking," I laughed. "How do you know?"

"This isn't the first time she's done this," he said proudly.

"What's your location?" I asked.

"Just get to the nearest outcropping on the mountain and I'll meet you there," Tu'ver instructed before disconnecting.

"I'm going to meet up with Tu'ver, then locate the human women," I announced to whoever was nearby.

I wasn't in the mood for going through the chain of command. Knowing Mariella had caused that rockslide made me feel better.

Teisha was likely with her, meaning she was out of harm's way.

For now.

The climb up to the nearest outcropping was easy. Tu'ver was already there, waiting for me and patiently cleaning his sniper rifle.

"That looked rough," he tutted when he saw me.

"It was," I replied. "The Gorgos were assisting combat."

"What?" Tu'ver brow furrowed. "Were the fanatics going mad?"

"No," I shook my head. "It was like the Gorgos were offering guidance in battle, rather than taking over completely."

"That's unsettling," he frowned. "I'm not sure what to make of that."

"Me, either," I shrugged. "Maybe the women have found something helpful in the mountain."

"Speaking of the mountain, any idea how to get back inside?"

"The archway we came out of is up there." I pointed straight up. The climb was going to be difficult, especially without any grappling equipment.

"We should've thought of this before sliding down the mountain like fools," Tu'ver sighed.

"We should've," I agreed. "If the women ask, we were definitely smart enough to plan this far ahead."

TEISHA

I surveyed our handiwork with a grin.

"I can't believe that worked!"

"I just hope our soldiers had the good sense to pay attention to our comms message," Mariella muttered.

My face went pale.

"You don't really think any of our guys were buried in the rocks, do you?" I asked.

"No," she reassured me. "In fact, I doubt many of the enemy jerks were crushed to death, either. My goal was to cause chaos, not a massacre."

"That makes me feel a little better."

"If someone down there saw the rockslide and decided not to get out of its way, I can't be held responsible for that," Mariella shrugged. "That's just poor decision making on their part."

"I'm starting to think people have it wrong when they call Leena the scary sister," I joked.

"You're right about that." Mariella winked and flounced back to the archway in the mountainside. "Shall we go check on our men?"

"Yes." I scrambled over loose rock, careful not to start another slide. "I'd like to verify that both Sa'lok and Tu'ver are smart enough to move out of the way of a rockslide."

"I feel like that's a good entry-level requirement for a relationship," Mariella chuckled.

"I'll make sure Sa'lok knows what's expected of him."

"So, you've decided you're in a relationship with him now?" she prodded.

I sighed heavily as I switched on my flashlight.

"I have more important things to worry about than arbitrary labels to describe the social interactions between Sa'lok and me."

"Did you mean social or did you mean sexual?" she waggled her eyebrows.

"Were you saving that line for a special occasion?" I quipped.

"Nope. I made it up on the spot. You're welcome."

"My point is, I'm not labeling anything until we're off this damn mountain of mystery," I said with a decisive nod.

"That's fair. Do you have anything to mark the walls with?"

"What for?" I asked.

"I don't want to explore the same length of the tunnel over and over again. If we mark the wall, we'll know we've been here and that we should choose another path when we come back through."

"Smart," I nodded. "But no, I don't have anything. If you have a knife, we can use blood."

"Goodness me," Mariella wrinkled her nose. "I'm not that desperate to mark up a wall."

"Well, excuse me!" I chuckled. "I was trying to be helpful."

"Helpful? More like creepy," Mariella laughed.

We chit-chatted back and forth as we made our way to the lower part of the mountain. It wasn't long before we heard the rumbling sounds of deep, familiar male voices in the tunnel ahead.

"Sa'lok?" I called out.

"It's the ghost of Sa'lok," Sa'lok called back.

"Damn," I swore. "I was really hoping that rockslide would've taken you out for good."

He appeared in the beam of my flashlight, grinning from ear to ear.

"You'll have to try harder than that to get rid of me."

Acting on my new resolution not to feel weird about expressing affection for Sa'lok, I ran up to him and threw my arms around his neck. His muscular arms slid around my waist as he pulled me in close.

"Did you discover anything new while I was gone?" he asked once we broke apart.

"No, but we're about to go explore the tunnels we haven't covered yet."

"How will you tell the difference?" he asked. "Did you mark them in blood or something?"

"Funny! Leaving a blood trail was my first thought too, but Mariella was having none of it."

"You're both creepy!" Mariella shouted from further up the tunnel, where she was checking Tu'ver over for injury.

"Thank you," Sa'lok called back. "I've worked hard to become so."

Mariella looked like she wanted to say something back, but before she could get any words out, the ground beneath our feet began to tremble.

"Is that another rock slide?" I shouted.

"I don't think so," Tu'ver replied. "It feels like it's coming from inside the mountain, not on top of it."

"Shit," I swore. "It could be a cave-in."

"Stay close," Sa'lok urged.

He tucked me under his arm and took a step toward Mariella and Tu'ver.

A slab of rock shot straight up through the floor of

the tunnel. The last thing I saw before it completely closed us off was Mariella's pale, frightened face.

"What the hell?" I coughed when the dust settled.

"Did that rock rise through the floor?" Sa'lok sputtered. "You saw that, right?"

"I did." I placed my palm flat against the slab that now separated us from Mariella and Tu'ver. Part of me expected my hand to go right through it as if it was nothing more than a trick of light and shadow.

"Sa'lok, come in!" Sa'lok's comms unit crackled.

"Tu'ver, do you read me?"

"Yes. Are you all right?"

"We're not injured, just confused," Sa'lok replied. "What about you?"

"We're fine. We think our end of the path leads out of the mountain. We'll head out and regroup. The strike teams are still in the area."

"Copy that. We'll find a way out and join you when we can."

The comms unit clicked off.

"You have a real knack for getting trapped in caves, don't you?" I joked in an attempt to hide the fear that was slowly taking hold.

"We all have our unusual talents," Sa'lok smirked.

He reached out for me in the darkness. This time, I didn't feel at all strange about seeking comfort with him. He wrapped me in his arms, his chin resting gently on the top of my head.

"At least we'll have a chance to explore," I said.

"Exactly. Who knows? Maybe we'll solve the mystery of this place on our way to finding a way out."

"If only," I sighed wistfully. I wasn't a fan of being inside the mountain before, but I could bear it, knowing I had some idea of where the exits were. Now, that wasn't the case. With each step, I felt my heart rate increasing.

"Your pulse doesn't feel normal," Sa'lok frowned.

"Oh," I laughed awkwardly. "I was really hoping you wouldn't notice that."

"Are you well? Human hearts can only beat so fast for so long," he said. "I don't want your heart to pop."

I held back a laugh.

"Pop?" I asked, fighting a smile.

"I heard that human hearts can explode when they're put under too much strain."

My sides started aching with the effort it took to stop myself from laughing. I couldn't laugh at Sa'lok, not when he was looking at me with such earnest concern.

"No," I said, though my voice came out high and tight.

"Why are you talking like that?" he asked. "Is your heart okay?"

"Where did you learn that human hearts pop?" I squeaked.

"I've heard humans say so many times," he said. "Why are you looking at me like that?"

"Like what?" I asked.

"Like you're underwater and running out of oxygen."

I couldn't hold my laughter back any longer.

"I'm sorry," I cackled as I gasped for breath. "That was just too damn funny."

"I don't understand." Sa'lok still looked so concerned which, of course, only made me laugh harder. "Is excessive laughter a sign of a deeper heart problem?"

"There's nothing wrong with my heart." I placed my hands on his shoulders reassuringly.

"Why are you crying?"

I pulled one hand away from him and touched my cheek. Sure enough, I found tears.

"I'm just laughing too hard," I explained. "You've never seen a human laugh so hard they cry?"

"Humans do that?"

He looked so concerned. I felt terrible as another round of laughter took me.

"Yes, humans do that," I said when I caught my breath. "Human hearts don't explode, either. It's an expression we use for a lot of things. I once saw a puppy so cute I thought my heart would explode. See?"

"Not really," he shook his head. "Did your pulse also climb to an unsettling rate when you saw said puppy?"

"Probably not," I admitted. "My pulse is so high now because I'm afraid."

"Yet you're laughing?"

"Humans go completely haywire when we're scared enough," I said. "You should've noticed that by now."

"You needn't be scared," he assured me.

"I'm lucky your circuits glow the way they do. I'd be way more scared without that light."

"But you have a light of your own," he pointed out.

"I know," I shrugged. "But, for some reason, the glow of your circuits makes me feel better. Safer."

"Glad I could help," he smiled in the dark and held out his hand for me. I took it.

"So, hearts don't explode?" he asked once we were walking again.

"No," I laughed softly. "But it can feel like they're going to."

"Humans have odd bodies," Sa'lok said thoughtfully.

"Should I take offense to that?" I snorted.

"No!" He whirled to face me, looking frantic. "Your body is amazing. I adore your body. There's nothing odd about it."

"Watching you panic is fun," I grinned.

His frantic looked faded the moment he realized I was teasing him.

"You're cruel," he smirked.

"Maybe," I shrugged. "But the more I tease you, the less worried I am about being trapped in a mountain temple for all of eternity."

"Is it a temple?" He tilted his head to one side.

"I'm not sure," I admitted. "I haven't found anything to indicate what this place was used for."

"Tu'ver thought it might be residential," he offered. "Simply because it looks nothing like the other sites."

"His guess is as good as mine at this point," I sighed.

"While we're stuck in here, we might as well look for clues," Sa'lok offered. "If anything, it'll help keep your mind busy."

"Good idea," I said, my eyes lingering on a wall of unreadable text. I wished I knew what it said.

I also wished there was something to be done about the growing buzzing sensation in my head.

Because the deeper we went, the louder it became.

SA'LOK

I kept an eye on her as we walked.

We trudged through the darkness slowly, careful not to step on loose rocks, and went further into the mountain.

The tunnels were like a maze, snaking through the rock with no clear direction, and there were so many twists, side passages and turns that it was almost impossible to keep track of our path.

"How are you feeling?" I asked Teisha. She had grown silent, her usual teasing and snark giving way to the sound of ragged breathing. Jewels of sweat gleamed on her forehead, plastering locks of hair to her skin as they trickled down her face.

"I'm fine," she replied, but her tone was clipped and tense. She was lying. Stopping, I turned to her and laid the back of my hand against her forehead. "I said I'm fine," she insisted, swatting my hand away.

As she did it, she swayed back like a drunkard and had to place one hand against the wall for support.

"You're running a fever, Teisha." The heat coming off her body was so strong that I could feel it from where I was standing. "I think it's better we sit down for a moment and catch our breaths."

"Are you tired? You don't need to use me as an excuse if you want to rest," she threw at me, a sardonic grin tugging at the corners of her parched lips. Clearing her throat, she pushed herself off the wall and tried to keep on walking, but her knees buckled. She fell forward, the palms of her hands ready to meet the floor, but I caught her before she landed.

"Sit down," I told her, and this time she didn't argue with me. Breathing hard, she leaned back against the wall and slid to the ground. Her body was starting to go limp, and I could tell she was struggling with something as simple as sitting down.

Placing my hand on the nape of her neck, I helped her lie down, using my backpack as an improvised pillow.

"I'm sorry, Sa'lok," she breathed out, her voice feeble and weak. Her clothes were drenched in sweat, and her lips were so dry they had already started to crack. Even her skin was starting to turn pale. "Let me just catch my breath for a minute and then we'll continue."

"Don't worry about it," I whispered, our voices echoing throughout the darkness of the tunnels. "We can take as much time as you need, alright? We're not in a hurry." She nodded weakly, her eyes closed.

"I just feel so goddamn tired." She ran the tip of her tongue over her parched lips, and I immediately went for my backpack and grabbed the small canteen I had brought with me.

Carefully holding her head up, I held the canteen to her lips. She took a couple of gulps, and then coughed awkwardly as I laid her head back down. "And my head...God, my head feels like it's gonna pop."

"Human bodies don't pop like that, remember?"

"Yeah," she smiled faintly. "But this headache...it's killing me. It feels like there's a swarm of wasps inside me, buzzing and buzzing and—"

"I know." Sitting beside her, I laid my hand on top of hers and gave it a squeeze. While her face was burning up, her hands were as cold as ice.

Not a good sign.

She had been fine an hour ago—how was it possible for her to get this sick in such a short time?

In the back of my mind, though, I knew that she wasn't sick. I was just trying not to think of it.

I didn't want to face reality.

"I think...I think it's better if you keep on walking," she whispered faintly. "Find a way out, and then you can come back for me. I just don't think I'll be able to keep up, you know?"

"Hey," I replied, stroking her cheek with my hand. "I'm not gonna leave you."

"You're too good," she continued, and her eyelids fluttered open. She didn't look at me, though. She just looked straight up at the curved ceiling of the tunnel, her gaze focused on something I couldn't see.

That was when I noticed it.

The green in her eyes was fading, a sickly gray taking its place. It looked like a blotch of paint someone had dropped on a pool of clear water, and it had already started to take over the white of her eyes, as well.

My heart sank.

Teisha was infected, and there was nothing I could do about it.

"I'm sorry," I whispered, even though by now I was no longer sure if she could hear me. She was slipping in and out of consciousness, her eyes open but devoid of that spark of intelligence I had grown so accustomed to. "If only I had brought some of the serum with me, maybe I could..." I trailed off then, a knot forming in my throat.

Why hadn't I brought the serum with us? We had

tested it on Teisha, sure, but she hadn't been infected at the time.

There was no reason to believe it would work right now, or was there? I knew the personnel in Glymna had been tasked with trying it out on the infected scientist, but they had been waiting for a sample from the Nyheim lab.

Not that any of it mattered.

We were lost inside the belly of an ancient mountain, and the serum was not a part of the equation. Leaning back against the wall, I ran one hand through Teisha's hair and exhaled sharply.

Was this going to be it?

Was I going to lose her?

"I'm so fucking sorry," I pushed past gritted teeth, looking down at the expressionless mask her face had turned into. "I shouldn't have let you come here. This is all my fault."

By now, she was no longer blinking, her eyes now all a pale gray, no trace of green in them. It was as if whatever was inside her was slowly eating away at her very soul, devouring who she was, feeding off of it.

"I love you, Teisha," I continued, taking her hand in mine. Her delicate fingers rested against the palm of my hand, motionless. "Ever since the first day I saw you...I've always loved you."

It was the truth—the first time I'd laid eyes on her

freckled skin, those tiny dimples forming on the corners of her mouth whenever she laughed, I knew I had found *her*. I didn't have a name for it at the time, but now I did.

It was love, pure and unbridled.

"You're my best friend, Teisha," I continued, the words simply pouring out of me. "After we crash landed here, I spent every waking minute trying to figure out a way to leave. I wanted to go back home, you see? I only stopped thinking of it when you stepped into my life. After that, a life here started making sense."

I bit my bottom lip, hard enough to draw blood. "And after what happened last night..." I shook my head, struggling to find the right words. "I was looking forward to building a life here. A life *with you*. Because, without you, nothing makes sense, not anymore."

I closed my eyes and rested my head against the rock. I didn't know what I was feeling anymore. It was love, but it was rage, too.

Powerlessness. For the first time in my life, I knew exactly what I wanted, and it was being taken away from me.

"Sa'lok," she whispered softly, and her fingers twitched against the palm of my hand. "Sa'lok..." I sat up, my heart kicking against my ribcage. Looking down at her face, I found her eyelids fluttering, a spark of green flickering through the gray haze that had taken over her eyes.

"I'm right here," I said, my voice fraught with emotion. "I'm right here, Teisha." Leaning in, I gently kissed her forehead, her cheeks, her chin.

I cupped her face with my hands and rested my forehead against hers. "Come back to me. This life...it only makes sense with you around."

"Sa'lok..." she repeated, and brought her hands up to mine. The green in her eyes was becoming brighter now, and I could see the gray mist clouding her gaze slowly fading. She was fighting against the Gorgos.

By everything that's sacred and holy, she was putting up a fight.

"That's it." Cradling her against my chest, one hand supporting her head, I looked straight into her eyes. "Fight, Teisha. Just keep fighting."

My heart was beating fast, but now there was hope fueling it.

Against all odds, Teisha was resisting.

TEISHA

It was difficult to stay calm. I knew something was
wrong with me. At first, I couldn't link my
thoughts together. It was like my brain had been dipped
in cold molasses. Sa'lok knew something was
wrong, too.

The moment he looked me in the eye, I understood.

Nothing else would cause that level of alarm in his
eyes.

A Gorgo had somehow latched on to me and was
trying to take my mind.

Not a chance in hell.

The problem was, deep down I knew how to fight
them off, but I couldn't make the thoughts cooperate in
my head.

My inner voice turned to gibberish. Sa'lok's name

was hard to call forward in my mind, even though I was staring him right in the face.

Somewhere in my mind, something urged me to be calm. I wasn't sure if it was my own instincts or the Gorgo, hoping to lull me into a false sense of security.

Movement caught my eye. It took me longer than it should have to realize the movement was a hand.

That hand was connected to an arm. That arm connected to a chest, a body, and a face. A man. No. An alien.

An important one.

Who was that?

I knew him.

I loved him.

Or did I?

I didn't know.

The hand that belonged to the handsome alien with a name I couldn't grasp touched my skin. I should've felt something more.

His touch felt more like a memory than a physical exchange.

It was harder to see now. There was a film over my vision, glassy and murky at the same time. Why did it hurt so much?

Why couldn't I blink?

I didn't know what to do.

"Hang on!" The other person's voice came through.

God, why couldn't I think of his name? I had to know his name. He was so important to me. I was sure of it.

"Help," I tried to speak but I wasn't sure if I said anything at all. Everything was so difficult. The smallest movements were exhausting. Even breathing became a challenge.

Something whispered against my consciousness. It wasn't a voice, exactly. It was more like a presence. It urged me to relinquish control. It promised that it would take care of everything, that I'd be able to rest.

That sounded so nice.

I just wanted to sleep.

My head snapped back twice. I realized hands were on my shoulders, but I could barely feel them. The alien male I was with was shaking me.

"Serum!" he shouted.

Or maybe he was whispering. I couldn't tell anymore. My ears felt overly sensitive but also as if they were stuffed with soaking wet cotton balls. My brain couldn't make heads or tails of the opposing sensations.

Serum?

The sounds my companion made finally clicked in my brain.

What serum?

The growing presence in my mind urged me to forget about it, to dismiss it as nonsense. But why?

Something harsh snapped in my head.

This time, I realized I wasn't being shaken.

The harsh mental rebuke was from the presence in my mind. Serum was a bad word, according to the presence.

A flash of memory hit me like a lightning strike.

The alien beside me, his name was Sa'lok. I remembered that now. He made something in a clean white room. He let me try it.

It made me feel wonderful.

The presence in my head stung my mind, trying to put me off my current train of thought. Clearly, it was important.

Or dangerous. Maybe it was trying to warn me. Why would it need to warn me about something that made me feel wonderful?

What was it?

"Serum!" Sa'lok shouted. I watched his mouth move. Surely, he was saying more than just one word. So many complicated mouth movements couldn't yield just one sound.

Serum was the word my brain chose to hear. If Sa'lok said it, it had to be important and safe. I didn't know how I knew, but I was certain he wouldn't put me in danger.

I focused on the serum, the lab, and the wonderful feelings I'd felt.

A face appeared in my mind's eye. A woman. She

was pretty. Not young, but not old, either. I knew her. I know I did. I felt that same sensation of familiarity I felt when I looked at Sa'lok.

Her name was buried in my consciousness. I tried to dig it out. The presence in my mind stopped me.

Gorgoxian.

That was the name that went with the presence in my mind. The name made me shudder. In my present state, I couldn't remember why a Gorgoxian was a bad thing.

I directed all of my efforts into focusing on the woman's face. My thoughts clicked into place.

Her name was Syra. She was my sister.

She had two children. Twins. Lyrie and Lyle. My family. I loved them.

Thoughts started flowing one after another as if I'd turned on a spigot inside my head.

Lyrie liked wearing my old aviator goggles. Lyle knew the inside of a plane almost as well as I did. Syra was always nervous when I took them flying. She was more practical than I, but I didn't mind. I stayed with her often. She was a great cook, though Lyrie and Lyle were picky eaters.

The best day of my life had been when they were born. Syra almost didn't survive, but she refused to quit on them. She was going to raise them, no matter what.

The Gorgoxian in my head attacked the bonds of

memory but to no avail. It couldn't destroy memories. It couldn't destroy love. I pushed back against it.

I loved my family. I loved flying. My grandma made amazing bread. I had a great job.

My best friend was an alien and I loved him with all my heart.

The presence in my head stumbled.

I had the idea of building a wall around my mind with memories. One after another, I called forth treasured memories, laying them down like bricks between myself and the Gorgoxian. Time didn't exist anymore.

Finally, it loosened its grip. It felt like a wet snake slithering out of my brain.

My head came into contact with something hard.

"Teisha?" Sa'lok's voice pierced my sensitive ears. I winced.

"What happened?" I rasped when I felt like I could control my voice again.

"A Gorgo tried to take you," he explained. "Open your eyes as wide as you can and look at me."

I did as he told me, though my eyelids felt heavy and stiff. He shone a light in my eyes, which hurt more than anything.

"I'm sorry," he soothed when I jerked my head away. "I'm just making sure your eyes are clear."

"What's the verdict, doctor?" I asked through gritted teeth.

"Your eyes are clear and lovely as ever."

Slowly, he helped me to my feet.

Apparently, I'd collapsed when the Gorgo fled my body. I'd skinned my knee at some point. It stung a little but it didn't compare to the throbbing pain in my head.

"How did you do it?" Sa'lok asked. "The Gorgo, I mean. How did you get rid of it? No one has survived it before."

"I heard you shouting 'serum' at me over and over," I said. "It took me a while to understand what you meant. The Gorgo muddled all my thoughts."

"What did you do when you worked it out?"

"I thought about happy memories," I explained. "My sister, the twins, my job. You."

"Me?"

"Yes." My cheeks grew hot as I blushed. I didn't know why I felt so embarrassed. "You're part of me, Sa'lok. You're more than a friend."

"You're more than my friend, too," he grinned and tucked a loose strand of hair behind my ear, and fire trailed through my skin at his touch.

"It's because of you that I was able to fight off the Gorgo," I confessed. "Thinking about how much I love you broke its hold."

"You love me?"

I couldn't bring myself to look at his face in case he wasn't happy.

"Yes."

"Teisha." He tipped my chin up, forcing me to look into his eyes. "I love you, too. I have for ages."

I wasn't sure what happened next. All I know was that I felt a surge of happiness, then I was kissing him, hungry, desperate for him, craving his touch.

Needing him.

"Are you sure?" he asked in a ragged whisper. "You've had a hell of an afternoon."

"Good memories," I murmured as I nipped at the strong line of his jaw. "I think it's important that we make some more good memories, right here, right now."

"As my mate desires," he growled, then fell upon me.

He backed me up against the wall. I felt the ridges and bumps of the carved texts against my back.

He kissed me hard. I kissed him back. I kissed him anywhere my lips could touch. My aching limbs didn't ache as badly when I was in his arms. My head no longer felt like it was in a fog.

Being so close to him was, somehow, restorative.

He cupped my ass with both hands, lifting me so I could wrap my legs around his waist. I felt the evidence of his arousal pressing against me through his pants.

My brain was still sluggish, even though I was driven to take him, to taste him as he ground against my core.

"Please, Sa'lok," I begged. "Now."

In a moment, he'd slid my shirt up, his strong hands kneading my breasts, pulling and teasing my nipples into hard buds.

In a smooth motion that should have taken my breath away with his strength, he lowered my pants while still holding me, then loosened his own belt.

But my breath was already gone, whisked away by his kisses.

"My Teisha," he growled against my throat as he slowly forced his thickness between my slick folds. "Mine."

"Yours," I gasped, as with a final thrust, he seated his full length inside me.

The back of his hand cupped my neck, preventing my head from bumping against the hard wall as he drove in and out of me.

For the second time that day, time lost all meaning. I could've stayed like that for hours, drowning in every pleasant sensation until the end of the universe. Each kiss lit a new fire in me. Each stroke of his cock sent a new wave of pleasure crashing through me.

When I reached the perfect peak of my pleasure, every nerve in my body was tuned to him. He didn't stop. He kept going until I went over the peak a second time.

Only then did he find his release.

I clung to him in the darkness. At some point, our light went out, but I didn't remember when. I traced the faintly glowing lines of his circuits.

Now that I had him, I'd never let him go.

SA'LOK

We lay in each other's arms, and we didn't say a word for a long time. We merely sat there and enjoyed the silence, the steady rise and fall of Teisha's chest all I needed to know that we were in the clear.

Clutching her hand in mine, I kissed her forehead and closed my eyes. It should've been impossible, but Teisha had warded off a Gorgo infection.

No serum, no cure, no anything. She used nothing but her sheer will to defeat the parasite inside her.

"How are you feeling?" I asked her, and this time I didn't feel a pang of anxiety as I waited for her answer. Slowly, she turned around and looked me in the eye, a smile drawn across her lips.

"Tired," she admitted. "But I feel good. I really do."

"You think you can walk?"

"Yeah, I think so." Laying one hand on my shoulder, she pushed herself up to her feet. She didn't stagger or sway.

She merely stood straight and looked around, her green eyes peering into the darkness ahead. "I feel alive," she continued, her smile widening. Offering me one hand, she helped me up to my feet and then patted the front of her jeans, tiny clouds of dust bursting into the air.

"It should've been impossible," I said, still trying to process all that had happened. "To fight off the Gorgo by yourself, it's..." I trailed off, not sure of the word I wanted to use.

My first impulse was to describe it as a miracle, but that would've been wrong.

Teisha had pulled through an unwinnable situation. It was possible her earlier exposure to the serum had acted as a form of inoculation.

Still, the credit was all hers.

"You were right, Sa'lok," she said. "Eliciting the right memories is the key to fighting off a Gorgo infection."

"Let's just hope the serum will have the same effect on the general populace," I said, thinking of Leena.

By now, she should already have produced a few batches of the serum. With some luck, we could be close to putting an end to the Gorgo epidemic. And it was high time that happened.

"You wrote the formula." Taking one step toward me, Teisha went on her tiptoes and brushed her lips against mine, the sweetness of her mouth enough to make my heart beat faster.

"It's going to work, Sa'lok. Trust me."

I answered her with a nod. Truth be told, right now the only thing I cared about was the fact that she was standing in front of me, her eyes and smile as bright as they had ever been.

"Now, let's get out of here, shall we?"

We kept on walking for the better part of an hour, cutting our way through the mountain as we looked for a way out. The tunnels, though, seemed to be going deeper and deeper, no alternative paths for us to take.

We tried a few of the bifurcations, careful to mark our route just so we didn't get lost, but it was useless— all paths seemed to lead deeper into the mountain's core. Not just that, but they were also sloping up at a steep angle, forcing us to move toward the peak.

Whoever had built this structure and carved these tunnels, had done so with the belief that something important was at the top.

"Does this mountain never end?" Teisha asked after another hour of walking, raking one hand over her face as she leaned against one of the walls.

By now, they had starting slanting inward, which meant we had to be close to the peak. I just hoped that my theory wasn't wrong, and that we weren't walking toward a dead-end.

"We should be close now," I replied, even though I didn't know exactly *what* we were close to.

Sucking in a deep breath, I grabbed my comms unit and tried it once more. All I got was static; the walls were simply too thick.

Usually that wouldn't be a problem, as K'ver comms units had been specifically designed to work anywhere, but something in this mountain seemed to be interfering with the electronics. "Come on, let's just keep going."

Leading the way, I kept on walking up the sloping path. The walls started narrowing in on us, and the ground angled up so much that I had to walk with both my hands on the walls just so I wouldn't slip.

Our pace was slow and tortuous, but we kept on going all the same.

"Look, up ahead," Teisha cried out from behind me, and I raised my eyes to see a faint glow in the distance. "Do you see it?" There was a narrow bend in the tunnel, and a warm light spilled from whatever was hiding at the end. Upping my pace, I held my breath as I navigated the curvature of the wall, then exhaled sharply as the narrow walls finally gave way to a spacious hollow chamber.

The walls here were smooth, as if someone had

polished them, and the ceiling had jagged, angular lines that culminated in a single point.

Runes had been carved into the smooth stone all around, with even the rock beneath our feet covered in that strange Gorgo script.

Those were just details, though. What really drew my attention wasn't the architecture, or the thousands of runes covering the chamber. No, what really got my attention was the blinding orb of light floating right at the center.

"What the hell?" Teisha muttered under her breath and, just like me, she shielded her eyes with the palm of her hand. It took us almost a minute for our eyes to adjust to the brightness, but once they did, Teisha started walking to the glowing orb.

"Careful," I said, placing a hand on her shoulder and stopping her. "We don't know what that is."

As I glanced at it once more, I realized the orb wasn't exactly solid. Thousands of minuscule flecks of light were floating around the same point, and it was from them that the brightness emanated.

"Can you feel it?" Teisha asked me, and I answered her question with a confused glance. I had no idea what she was talking about. Grabbing my hand, she pulled me toward the light, and that's when I felt it.

The tiny lights started swirling faster and faster, like wheels spinning around an invisible axis, and I felt a strange presence in my mind. It felt like there were bugs crawling underneath my thoughts, trying to unearth them.

"It's kinda like how it is with the Puppet Master," Teisha whispered. "Except it's different. I don't know how to put it."

She was right. The experience was eerily familiar to what someone felt whenever they stood too close to the Puppet Master's core. But while with the Puppet Master there was a feeling of warmth, right now I felt like sharp icicles were working their way into my brain.

It was uncomfortable, to say the least.

"Stand back." Yanking on Teisha's shoulder, I dragged her away from the light. The moment I did it, the bright sparks started moving around so fast that the light coalesced and turned into something solid.

I could almost feel the weight of that bright orb, the oppressiveness of it bearing down on my mind.

I didn't know what we were looking at, but one thing I knew for sure: we had to get the hell out of the chamber before it was too late.

The thing was, it was already too late. I was dragging Teisha back toward the tunnels when a deep rumbling voice filled the chamber's hollowness.

"*Hello, Teisha,*" it said, and I turned around to see the orb's brightness flickering with the same cadence of the words. "*It's been awhile since I've met someone like you.*"

TEISHA

"Teisha Jovansen," the voice continued, and the hairs on the back of my neck stood up on end. "*Step closer. Come into the light.*" I didn't exactly hear those words, but my brain processed them all the same.

There was sound, but it was coming straight from the depths of my mind.

Before I even knew what I was doing, I started walking toward the orb of light. I would've gone all the way, if it weren't for Sa'lok.

"Don't," he said, his fingers wrapping around my wrist.

"I've heard this voice before," I said, that buzzing sensation from before coming back to haunt me.

"*Yes, you have. You know me, child,*" the voice continued, except it wasn't *a* voice. It was the voice of thousands, endless living and breathing beings crammed into one self-aware conscience.

I had heard that same voice coming out of the mouths of those that had been possessed.

Somehow, I was talking to the Gorgoxians. *"You're full of surprises, Teisha Jovansen,"* it continued, and it each time it uttered my name, I felt like hooks were being sunk into my flesh. *"There aren't many capable of withstanding me. But you did, didn't you? You're special."*

"What do you want?" I asked, my voice trembling. "Why have you come here?"

"To claim what's rightfully mine," it replied, and there was spite in those words. Hatred. *"This universe used to be mine, long before you were born, and it shall be returned to me soon."*

My eyelids fluttered, and my eyes rolled into the back of my head. I went down on my knees, a wave of nausea crashing against me, and then I saw it—millions and millions of star systems, as many as there were grains of sand on the beach, stretching from one end of the universe to the other.

I saw the birth of life, the endless cycle of stars. I saw it all in my mind's eye.

"Teisha?" Sa'lok's voice came to me, but it was distant. "Please, talk to me."

I could feel him holding my hand, but at the same

time, it was as if we were standing on different sides of the continent.

Inside me there was a deep thrumming sound, and I saw as a blanket of darkness stretched across the universe, swallowing up whatever spark of consciousness it could find. It devoured it all, gorging on life, and it grew.

Oh, how it grew.

"You see? Long before humans drew their first breath, I was already old. I reigned supreme."

There was a thick layer of rage coating those words, and each one of them popped into my head like fireworks. A searing pain took over the back of my head, and I gritted my teeth on instinct.

"You won't deny me what's mine. No one will."

"You...you've been stopped before," I managed to breath out. Underneath all those images flashing through my mind, there was something the Gorgoxians didn't want me to see.

But it was there all the same, and I yanked on that secret thread of knowledge as hard as I could. The pain suddenly stopped, and I saw how life had spread across the stars, tiny seeds of consciousness pollinating the universe.

The Gorgoxians kept on spreading, too, but tiny lighthouses of life sprouted all the same, keeping the darkness at bay. "You are powerful, but there are others as powerful as you are."

"The Ohmex are insignificant," it bellowed, and I thought my head was going to burst open.

I opened my eyes, to see shadows dancing around the chamber, the orb of light turning red as blood, painting the walls with a murderous crimson. *"They'll fall, just like you all will."*

"What is it talking about, Teisha?" Sa'lok asked me, his eyes round with concern. He could hear the Gorgoxians, but it seemed like only I was seeing these visions of so long ago. "Who are the Ohmex?"

"The Puppet Master," I replied. "It's talking about the species the Puppet Master belongs to."

Swallowing my fear down, I looked back toward the light. "Why do you hate them so much? What have they ever done to you?"

"They exist."

It was a dry answer, but I could see it was the truth.

Somehow, the existence of something like the Puppet Master was deeply offensive to everything the Gorgoxians stood for.

The two of them couldn't co-exist.

"Ohmex thrive on freedom. They inspire it in life around them, setting it free to grow and die as it pleases. The universe wasn't meant to be a free place, child. It was born out of chaos, and only power will stop it from

returning to chaos. Not freedom. The universe is meant to be ruled."

"You're wrong," I cried out.

"Am I?"

There was an undercurrent of laughter in its tone, almost as if it was mocking me.

"Then why has freedom been yielding to power? I've traveled far, moving from planet to planet, and I've been sucking the Ohmex dry each and every time. They're dying. The freedom they love so much will be the end of them. All the sentient races they've allowed to prosper have turned their backs on them, and their power has been sapped. All those lives they've protected throughout the millennia...it was all for nothing. Their time is over."

"That's not true...that's a lie," I tried to say, but I was growing weaker.

The chamber seemed to be spinning around me, and I had to close my eyes so that I didn't throw up.

I could feel the invisible tendrils of the Gorgoxians' consciousness filtering into my mind, working hard to tear down whatever barriers I had in place.

"Don't fight it," the Gorgoxians whispered, and I saw all of my memories being blotted out by a dark shadow.

I tried to think of Syra and the twins, but the darkness had already gotten to them. In my mind, I saw nothing but an abandoned house, those I loved turned into dust.

Gritting my teeth, I thought of Sa'lok, remembering the warmth of his embrace, but I was at the end of my rope now—after fighting off the Gorgo once, I wasn't sure if I'd be able to keep the rest of them at bay a second time.

"Sa'lok, I don't know if I can fight it." I squeezed his hand as tightly as I could, my words coming out between raspy breaths.

The headache had spread from the back of my head to between my eyes, and I was struggling to think straight. Around my thoughts there was that maddening buzzing sensation, as if a million wasps were trying to stab my consciousness into submission.

"Yes, you can," he tried to say, but his voice was so distant. I felt him pull me up to my feet, but the disconnect between my body and brain was growing at an alarming rate now.

I was aware of what was happening around me, but at the same time, it was as if it was all happening to a different person.

"Don't give up on me, Teisha. You're strong, you can fight it off." Throwing one of my arms over his shoulders, Sa'lok turned his back to the orb of light and started dragging me out of the chamber.

"*You can't run,*" the Gorgoxians said, a thousand different voices erupting into laughter all at once. "*You can't escape me. No one can. You belong to me, every single one of you.*"

"Stop, please stop," I cried out, my brain feeling as it was about to explode. As gently as he could, Sa'lok laid me down on the floor. "I can't go on. I just can't. But you still have a chance. You can go now, and you can—"

"No, Teisha," he cut me short. "I'm not going anywhere." He didn't say it, but I could read in his eyes the words he left unspoken—*if this is the end of the road for you, it's the end of the road for me, as well.*

"I love you, Sa'lok," I managed to say. Cupping his face with both hands, I pulled him toward me and kissed his lips.

If Teisha Jovansen was going to be wiped from existence, I wanted her last memory to be of how sweet Sa'lok's lips were.

Closing my eyes, I finally surrendered to the fatality of it all.

This was the end, and it was—

Suddenly, the walls started to tremble.

I tried to keep my eyes open to see what was happening, but it was getting harder and harder to do.

The long shadows of oblivion were already closing in on me, and I was too weak to fight them off.

The last thing I remember seeing was a vine.

SA'LOK

Thick vines burst through the rock so fast they slammed themselves against the ceiling. Some were as thick as my torso, and they all seemed hell bent on tearing the whole place apart.

The thickest one jerked back like a whip, and then it launched itself against the Gorgoxian light orb. Right before it hit its mark, an invisible force pushed it back against one of the walls.

"Come, Teisha, let's get out of here," I said, but she was already unconscious. I just hoped it wasn't too late for her. Picking her up from the floor, I started heading toward the exit, but a few vines sprung up from the floor and blocked the way.

Then, just a couple of seconds later, the arched

ceiling of the tunnel in front of us collapsed. "Fuck," I muttered.

We had just lost our only way out, but on the other hand, if the Puppet Master hadn't stopped me, Teisha and I would be dead by now.

Turning on my heels, I watched as more vines burst out from the floor, all of them whipping hard at the crimson orb of light in the center of the chamber.

Despite the Puppet Master's best efforts, it didn't seem like he could reach the strange Gorgoxian consciousness—every time a vine closed in on it, the lights started swirling faster and faster, and bright sparks of it jumped out from the orb to swat the vines away.

"I need a little help here," I cried out, hoping for the Puppet Master to hear me.

I had no idea how he had found us, and I wasn't entirely sure if he had managed to shake off the Gorgo infection in its entirety...but I had to hope.

Without his help, we were as good as dead.

"*Run*," I heard his faint voice whisper inside my head, and only then did I notice a tiny little vine brushing against my wrist. "*As far as you can. Don't look back.*"

Right at that moment, the thickest vine started slamming itself against the wall, doing it over and over again.

The rock cut into the vine, green sap dripped down its length, but the Puppet Master just kept at it. He only stopped when the rock finally cracked, creating an opening that allowed for sunlight to filter into the room. *"Now, Sa'lok, go."*

I didn't hesitate.

Keeping my arms tight around Teisha's inert body, I made a run for it. My boots slammed themselves heavily against the ground, beads of sweat dripped down my forehead, and the only thing I could hear was the pounding of my own heart.

I didn't have much time—soon enough, the mountain would come crashing down around us.

The Puppet Master was locked in a vicious fight against the Gorgoxians, and there was no doubt in my mind that the two of them would stop at nothing to obliterate the other.

Doing it as carefully as I could, I slipped through the crack in the wall and took a deep breath as a cold breeze whipped at my skin.

Steadying myself against the outer wall of the mountain, I held onto Teisha as tightly as I could. We were standing on a tiny ledge, and the wrong movement would see us plunging to our deaths.

Thankfully, the Puppet Master had thought of that.

A vine as thick as a rope was hugging the mountain

wall, and all I had to do was hold on to it as I navigated the ledge.

Taking my time, I ignored the violent sound of the battle taking place just a few feet away from me and followed the vine onto a little trail.

"Thank you, my friend," I said, brushing my fingertips against the vine.

I didn't know if the Puppet Master could hear me, but I hoped so. After what I had seen inside that chamber, I didn't know if he'd survive the day.

As soon as we'd emerged from the mountain, my comms system burst with pings of previous notifications and demands for updates.

"Sa'lok reporting in," I answered on the general channel, "we're out, but can't see what's going on."

"The battle is over," Tu'ver answered through the clamor of responses. "Enemy forces have already been relocated, and other than you two, we're all clear of the location. What took you two so long? Find anything interesting in there?"

"It's a long story, but wherever you are, you may want to get farther away," I replied, then focused on my footing.

"Where are we?" I heard a frail voice ask, and I looked down to see Teisha staring at me. Her weak arms regained some of her strength, and she laced one around my neck. The green in her eyes remained unchanged, and that was a huge relief.

The Gorgoxians were probably so focused on the Puppet Master that they had forgotten about Teisha. "What happened?"

"The Puppet Master saved us," I told her, smiling at her look of surprise.

"He's alive?"

"He is," I nodded. "He's fighting against that thing inside the mountain."

At that, Teisha's lips turned into a thin straight line. Just like me, she knew the Puppet Master's odds weren't that great.

"Come on, we have to get out of here before the entire mountain comes crashing down," I continued, walking down the trail as fast as I could.

Judging from what I could see, we weren't that far from the place where Teisha had landed her hovercraft.

If we could get there, maybe we'd have a chance at surviving this.

"Right there," Teisha cried out, pointing toward the distance. I had to narrow my eyes, but I eventually saw what she was pointing at.

The fuselage of her hovercraft reflected the sunlight, just like a beacon, and I couldn't help but think of it as the lighthouse that would guide us to safety.

Fifteen minutes later, I was opening the hovercraft's back door. Still carrying Teisha, I entered through the cargo hold and made my way to the front.

"You'll have to pilot it, Sa'lok," she whispered, her fingernails digging into my biceps. "I'm too dizzy and weak to do it."

"Alright," I nodded. "I'll do it."

"Don't crash it, you hear me?" Her fingernails went deeper into my flesh, and I smiled as I realized she was giving me one of her usual warnings.

She was weak and disoriented, but she was the Teisha I had fallen in love with.

"I'll do my best."

Placing her in the co-pilot's seat, I fastened her seatbelt and then took my own seat.

Only then did I realize the task in front of me wouldn't be an easy one.

I didn't mind piloting different aerial units, but the problem with Teisha's hovercraft was that it had been fully customized by her, for her.

"Alright, what do I do?"

"Turn on the fuel pump first," she instructed me, pointing at the lever to my right. The moment I pulled on it, a liquid sucking sound filled the entire cockpit. "Now divert power from the main unit to the engines. You'll have to wait until it stabilizes and then—"

"I think I got it," I said, flicking a bunch of switches in rapid succession. I was working on instinct alone, but after seeing Teisha pilot this ship countless times, I was up to the task.

It took me less than a minute to have the engines roaring at their loudest, and then it was only a matter of pushing ourselves off the ground.

The ship swayed left as it started its ascent, but I quickly fixed that by turning on the ancillary thrusters.

"I don't want to pressure you," Teisha said from behind me, "but if I were you, I'd be hurrying up now."

"Oh, shit," I muttered, finally hearing the loud rumble of boulders coming down the mountainside. I looked through the viewport just in time to see an avalanche of rocks tear down everything in their path, the gigantic mountain walls finally succumbing to their own weight.

Pulling the yoke against me, I gritted my teeth as I forced the hovercraft up. I did it just in time to avoid being swept up by the mountain's collapse, colossal clouds of dust making it impossible to see anything around me.

Relying on the navigation instruments, I somehow managed to head us up into the blue skies and away from the battleground where the Puppet Master and Gorgoxians were fighting to the death.

"Do you see anything?" I asked Teisha.

She said something, but I didn't even hear what it was. My question had already been answered by the violent flash of red that emerged from the dust below us.

The Gorgoxian orb had grown in size, and now it throbbed with rage, pushing the dust away.

For a moment, I thought the Gorgoxians had triumphed.

I was wrong.

Thick vines emerged from the rubble almost at the same time, all of them going higher than I thought could be possible.

They all reached for the crimson orb, trying to encase it and snuff it out, but the Gorgoxians weren't going down without more fight.

The orb lashed out with red bolts of energy, forks of lighting hitting the green vines over and over again.

"That doesn't look good," I muttered. Carefully, I started heading us further away from what was now an open arena.

Despite my urgent curiosity about the result of the battle, I didn't want to get caught in the crossfire.

Two ancient and powerful aliens were going all out, and I didn't want to end up as a mosquito on their windshield.

"What is he doing?" Teisha whispered, her face pressed against the window. By now, thousands of vines had emerged from the rubble, so many that it seemed like an entire jungle was flying up toward the Gorgoxian orb.

A thunderstorm of red bolts tried to keep the vines at bay, but there were too many of them.

Relentlessly, the Puppet Master encased the Gorgoxian light and started tightening itself around it.

Crimson flashes escaped from the openings in the Puppet Master's trap, but they were growing weaker and weaker with each passing second.

"He won," I blurted out, barely believing it. "I can't believe it. The Puppet Master really did it, he—"

Suddenly, the red light coming from the Gorgoxians became so bright that the vines turned translucent, their green skin turning red for a moment. I stared at the scene with my jaw hanging, not sure what I was looking at.

When I finally realized what was about to happen, it was already too late.

The explosion was unlike anything I had ever seen, and the light coming from it blinded me almost immediately.

I fumbled awkwardly with the yoke, tilting it up and praying that some altitude would be enough to keep us safe, but it was useless.

The shockwave came fast and hard, and the hovercraft was rocked by it in an instant.

"Hold tight," I cried out, the seat belt digging into

my flesh. We spun around like a piece of paper blown away by a tornado, and the hovercraft only slowed down after diving straight into the forest below us.

A thousand branches softened our crash landing, some of them swatting the viewport mercilessly, and I just hoped none of them would break through and impale us.

When we finally came to a stop, I had a hard time believing we were alive.

But we were.

Against all odds, we had survived.

TEISHA

"Help me into the chair," I begged Sa'lok.

"It may take a moment," he replied. "To do that, I'd have to move my shoulder, which I can't do."

"You moved your shoulder just fine before breakfast," I countered.

"And I'm paying the price for it now." Sa'lok flopped gracelessly into his seat.

I had no choice but to follow suit.

Every inch of my body felt like one big bruise. Three of my ribs were fractured, my wrist was sprained, my right thigh was basically purple from where it was smashed against the side of my hovercraft, and I was covered in a colorful array of sores, scrapes, and tender spots.

Thankfully, I wasn't concussed and other than my

ribs, nothing was broken. Recovery wouldn't take long. Hot baths were a must.

Sa'lok had dislocated his shoulder when the hovercraft crashed. It was still swollen and tender. Dr. Parr had to strap his arm down since he kept trying to move it before it was healed. There was a cut above his brow. I'm not sure what caused it, but it needed stitches.

Frankly, I thought he looked rather handsome with a scar. His ankle had been crushed by the side of the hovercraft smashing inward.

Unfortunately, it was broken, but K'ver bones healed quickly. I thought their augmented tech was only in their skin, but I was wrong. It was in their bones, as well.

He'd be walking around normally long before I could.

"Want to know something funny?" I leaned over and whispered in his ear. Twisting my body to face him was a difficult feat.

My ribs groaned in complaint. I couldn't do anything without my ribs making their opinion and discomfort known.

"What?" Sa'lok's eyes glinted with mischief.

"I've been hurt more times in the last two days than I have in my entire life," I replied.

"How is that funny?" He tilted his head to one side,

then immediately regretted the motion.

"I've spent more time with you in the last two days than we have over the course of our friendship," I said. "Coincidence? I think not."

"Oh, I see how it is," he chuckled. "Blame me for your clumsiness."

"Clumsiness?" I blurted.

"I've never been caught in so many rockslides and cave-ins before," he went one. "You're the common factor there."

"You caught me," I rolled my eyes, biting back laughter. "This was all just an elaborate ruse to drop a mountain on you."

"I knew it!"

I chuckled then winced, placing a hand against my aching side.

"Don't make me laugh," I whimpered.

"Don't make me smile." He gestured to the stitches above his brow, which flexed and stretched every time he smiled.

"Don't smile with your whole face," I cautioned him.

In response, he gave me a bland smile that was more of a grimace.

"Like that?"

"General Rouhr's almost here," Tu'ver announced as he entered the room.

Sa'lok and I straightened up as best we could and tried to appear professional in our injured states.

Within a few seconds, I had to slump back down in my seat. It hurt too much to hold myself upright.

The general strode into the room. I was used to him always looking worn down, but this was a new extreme.

He looked like he hadn't slept in days. He must've just returned from the field. His hair was still covered in a fine layer of dust and his clothes were stained and tattered.

"I've just returned from the crater in the desert," he explained. "Those of you who have been there know what it usually looks like. I'm here to report that the crater has changed considerably."

"Is the Puppet Master alive?" A woman I didn't know asked. She wore a lab coat and a worried expression. She must work with Mariella's sister.

I knew I was surrounded by the best and brightest in General Rouhr's company. I struggled to wrap my head around the fact that I was one of them now. Who knew?

"As far as we can tell, he's alive," the general nodded. "But he's unresponsive. His condition is somewhat like a coma. Fighting the force of the Gorgoxians drained him. He's retreated into himself to heal."

"How badly was he hurt?" I asked.

"It's difficult to say. It's not as if we can examine the Puppet Master's entire body," he explained. "There's no way to tell how much of the damage is physical and how much is mental. From the reports of the incident at the mountain, I'd wager most of the damage was to the Puppet Master's mind."

"Where does that leave us?" a burly Valorni asked.

"We haven't seen any signs of Gorgo activity since the incident at the mountain," General Rouhr explained. "We've all learned to think of the Puppet Master as the beating heart of this planet. The temple scribblings led us to consider the mountain as the home of thought, the brain. The only way I can explain what happened in terms even remotely understandable is that the Puppet Master poured his heart into eradicating the brain of the Gorgoxians."

"That's not at all confusing," Sa'lok said under his breath.

Thankfully, the general didn't hear him.

General Rouhr spoke in terms that were largely abstract, but I believed I understood what he meant.

"The Puppet Master fought that battle for us," the general went on. "I believe he did it not only to save his own life, but to preserve the planet we all call home. His loyalty is to us and we'll be forever grateful for that."

"Do you think he'll come out of the coma soon?" a redhead with a serious brow asked.

"There's no way of knowing," General Rouhr shrugged. "The Puppet Master was in a state of hibernation for centuries before the Xathi crash disturbed him. It's possible we might never hear from him again in our lifetimes or even our children's lifetime."

"That's sad," another woman murmured. "I feel like I've lost a friend."

"And an ally," a Skotan added.

"We would've been lost long ago if it weren't for the Puppet Master."

"I don't think we were ever meant to be involved," Sa'lok spoke up. Everyone turned to look at him, perplexed.

"The Puppet Master made it no secret that he was of an ancient race," Sa'lok continued. "He told us the Gorgoxians were even older than he was. We've been acting like we had any control in the situation. I think we lost what little control we might have had long ago."

"So, you're saying we shouldn't have gotten involved in the first place," a Valorni snapped.

"Not at all," Sa'lok shook his head. "On the contrary, we needed to be involved for the sake of the people who are alive today. But I think we should stop pretending we were ever a fighting force on this planet. After the Xathi were dealt with, we became nothing more than potential collateral damage between two ancient forces we can never hope to understand."

I reached out and took his hand.

"It was never about us," I supplemented. "We just happened to stumble into their war."

"Exactly." The corners of Sa'lok's mouth twitched up into a smile. "There's no point in trying to understand everything that happened, because we aren't capable of understanding it. We're just lucky one of the key players had a big enough heart to consider our well-being."

"If anything, the Puppet Master managed to cleverly weaponize us," Tu'ver said. "He could've strong-armed us into being his mindless soldiers, but he didn't. He worked with us so we'd work with him."

"We'll never know how deep the conflict between the Puppet Master's race and the Gorgoxians ran," I said. "Maybe that's a good thing. Maybe we couldn't handle it if we knew."

"An interesting viewpoint," General Rouhr nodded. "But that doesn't mean our work is done."

"Of course not," Sa'lok agreed.

"With the Puppet Master in a state of deep hibernation," the general continued, "we don't know how much he'll be able to do by way of maintaining the planet. That's something we can do for him."

"We owe him that much," I murmured.

Everyone in the room seemed to be in agreement.

"Where do we start?" Sa'lok asked.

"We've already started," General Rouhr said. "We've figured out how to sustain our population while doing as little damage as possible. Now, we will turn to the humans for guidance, as they have turned to us."

"The humans?" Mariella asked softly.

"Yes." The general awarded her with a rare smile. "Before we arrived, you humans knew exactly how to live as part of the ecosystem."

"We were a far cry from the top of the food chain," Leena pointed out. "Just about everything in the jungle can kill us."

"That's no matter," he said dismissively. "We don't need to dominate this planet. We need to integrate ourselves into it."

"I don't follow," Leena said.

"We have to find a way to become part of this planet in the same way the Puppet Master has. We're simply living on top of it. We don't contribute to the way it survives, but we use it to ensure our survival."

"So, what? Are we official Planet Keepers now?" a Valorni joked.

"Yes," General Rouhr said brightly. "That's exactly what we'll be until the Puppet Master comes back to us."

SA'LOK

"One more batch done," Leena announced proudly, hands on her hips as she looked down at the container on the table. In it were close to one hundred vials, all of them filled with the synthetic serum I had devised.

"It's still too early to celebrate," I teased her, even though I was proud of how fast we were producing the serum. We were getting better at it with each passing day. "We still need to do two more batches before we can call it a day."

"Let's make it four," she laughed happily, and then sealed the container and signed off on it. "We make a great team, Sa'lok."

"You bet we do."

Leena was a consummate professional when it

came to everything that happened inside the lab, and she was the most perfect research partner anyone could have.

Obsessed with improving the serum, she'd tweaked my formula until the result became almost immediate, and then she'd devised a production method that ensured we'd be able to deliver at least a thousand vials on a daily basis.

More than just that, she also knew when to crack a joke and how to keep things lighthearted. And after all the things I had been through, lighthearted was exactly what I needed.

I still dreamt of it sometimes, that violent battle of wills when the Puppet Master had faced off against the Gorgoxians.

It was odd, in a way—those two had been battling it out since forever, and I had been there to witness their final confrontation. Some people said I had been lucky to see it firsthand, but I wasn't so sure. Shit, if only people knew how close the Gorgoxians had been to victory.

Thankfully, that day hadn't ended in tragedy. The Puppet Master sacrificed himself, but the world woke up the next day to see the sun rising over the horizon.

The Gorgoxians withdrew from the planet, their presence fading until it became non-existent, and all the infected turned into husks. Their primal rage abandoned them, and they became nothing but empty shells.

We were worried, those first few days.

We came across so many of the infected, all of them as docile as sheep, but they weren't acting like humans at all. They didn't speak or react to anything that happened around them, and they sure as hell didn't seem to remember anything about their past lives.

Thankfully, the serum seemed to work on them. Just a few drops under their tongues and all we had to do was wait for a couple of minutes.

I never got tired of watching vacant eyes suddenly start to shine with that human smartness I had come to appreciate.

In a way, it was funny. The first few days on this planet, I never really cared much for the humans.

My mind had been set on the Xathi, and their destruction was the only thing that mattered to me.

Then I came across Teisha, and everything changed. I came to love the obstinate, stubborn humans and everything they stood for.

Maybe that was why the Puppet Master was so willing to sacrifice himself. He saw all the life on his planet, and he deemed it worthy. And I had to agree— for all their faults, the humans were worthy.

"What's up with you?" Leena elbowed me suddenly. "Spacing out during work hours?"

"Sorry," I cleared my throat. "I was just thinking of something."

"Yeah, I bet." Looking straight at me, she shook her head and rolled her eyes. "Hot date tonight, right?"

"What?"

"Oh, c'mon, Sa'lok," she laughed. "Don't be such a prude. I know you and Teisha are going out tonight. She enlisted Mariella to go shopping with her. Apparently, she wants to buy a dress, if you can believe it. Rumor has it that nobody has ever seen Teisha wear a dress."

"Really?" I had never thought of it, but it seemed like it was the truth. I knew Teisha better than anyone else in Nyheim, and I had never seen her wear a dress, or even a skirt. Now, though, it seemed like that was about to change.

"Lucky you, huh?" Leena continued, poking me with her elbow once more. Blood rushed to my cheeks, and I just looked down and started working on the next batch of the serum. I liked the women I worked with, but I still hadn't learned how to deal with their tendency to do what the dictionary defined as 'gossiping'.

I said nothing, hoping that would be enough for Leena to drop the matter, but it didn't seem like she was going to give up.

"Hey, Sa'lok, remember what I told you about Teisha? That dress thing?"

"Yeah?"

"Well, seems like I was right," she said, and then she grabbed my head with both hands and forced me to look up. My jaw dropped, my heart doing a somersault inside my chest.

"Hi there," Teisha smiled as she stepped into the lab. She was wearing a black cocktail dress that embraced her curves in the most perfect ways, the fabric clinging to her body like a second skin.

Her lips were scarlet and ripe, and there was just a faint hint of smoky makeup on her eyes. As for her hair, it had been straightened out and fell over her shoulders like a curtain of gold.

In short, she looked amazing.

"I don't even know what to say," I admitted. Putting the vial in my hands back on my workstation, I crossed the room and placed my hands on her hips. I looked straight into her green eyes as I leaned in and kissed her, our lips eager for a dance.

"You look beautiful, Teisha."

"I gotta say, it doesn't feel that bad to be wearing a dress," she admitted with a whisper. "Now, do you think Leena will let you out of the lab? I know it's still early, but—"

"Oh, get out of my lab, you two," Leena laughed,

shaking her head as she looked at us. "You guys are flooded with hormones. Go get rid of 'em somewhere else, I don't want you contaminating my lab."

"Well, you heard her," I smiled.

"You bet I did."

And that was it.

Arm-in-arm with Teisha, I walked out of the lab and into the rest of my life.

TEISHA

My status as an auxiliary pilot was elevated to that of a fully ranked captain. I was on the regular payroll, had a keycard, and had access to the entire aerial fleet.

None of General Rouhr's ships could compare to my hovercraft, though.

I offered up my first week's pay in exchange for having my beloved hovercraft returned to me and placed in a shop where I could fix her up. The general agreed and swiftly sent soldiers to get the task done.

Now that I think about it, I probably could've negotiated a better deal. But, at least I had my hovercraft back.

In addition to securing my air vessel, General Rouhr graciously gave Sa'lok and me some much-needed time off. Eager to get away from anything that reminded us of work, mountains, and the Puppet Master, we went to my sister's house.

Syra wasn't sure what to think about the idea at first. She didn't like anything she didn't have absolute control over. Luckily, Lyrie and Lyle took to Sa'lok right away.

He sat on the floor with them now, showing them how to build something out of twigs and dried leaves. The children were loving every moment of it.

"I never expected you to bring home a man," Syra said to me as we stood in her small kitchen. I carefully stirred a thick, creamy soup on the stove while Syra peeked in the oven to check on the bread she was baking.

"I didn't," I winked.

She rolled her eyes.

"I'm just not sure about this whole thing." She cast a look over her shoulder at Sa'lok and the children.

Lyrie settled herself in his lap, content to watch while Lyle clumsily rearranged whatever project he and Sa'lok were working on.

Every so often, Sa'lok would reach up and absentmindedly brush Lyrie's wild hair away from her face.

"What whole thing?" I asked carefully. "The alien thing?"

"What?" Syra looked at me in confusion. Her eyes widened when she realized my meaning. "Oh, goodness! No. I don't care about the alien thing. I'm worried about you."

"Why?" I tilted my head.

"You never brought a man home before," she said. "You didn't even have a romantic interest in this one until a few weeks ago. It just seems rather sudden."

"I know it might seem that way," I said. "But it's not. I've had feelings for him for a while. I just made the mistake of trying to put them off for a more convenient time."

"Oh," Syra chuckled. "That was foolish of you. You can't put those kinds of feelings off."

"I know that now," I replied. "Though, in my defense, the constant threat of death from an aggressive alien lifeform kept me fairly busy."

"Excuses, excuses," Syra tutted. "Don't stop stirring. It'll get lumpy."

I realized my hand on the ladle had gone still. I was too busy watching Sa'lok. It was nice watching him play with Lyrie and Lyle.

I had danced around the question of wanting children my whole life, but now that I saw him with the twins, children seemed more appealing.

"Speaking of aggressive aliens," Syra drew my attention back to her. "How's work coming?"

"Technically, I have time off," I said.

She snorted.

"Since when do you take time off?"

"Exactly," I grinned and pulled a miniature datapad out of my back pocket.

The screen glowed with messages from Mariella, Alyssa, Maki, and Amira, my new coworkers. I'd joined their loosely formed research team.

They each had some kind of anthropological background. I fit right in with them.

"Remember those things that were taking over people's bodies in Einhiv?" I asked.

"How could I forget? Cousin Marsha lives there," she said.

"Oh, right." I blushed. I'd completely forgotten about Cousin Marsha. "Is she okay?"

"As far as I know. I sent a message the day before yesterday. Haven't heard anything back."

"That's not unusual," I shrugged. "Isn't Cousin Marsha part of that holistic living group? No tech, no medicine, no modern conveniences?"

"Yes, but I figured she'd have the good sense to leave us a way to contact her," Syra huffed. "But, go on. What about the body-snatching aliens?"

"Well, we believe they erected temples last time they visited this planet."

"Last time?" Syra balked. "What is this? A vacation planet for them?"

"I hope not," I chuckled. "Anyway, there's writing all over the temples but it's a dead language. Hardly anyone has info on it. We're trying to translate it."

"Any luck?"

"Let me put it this way," I smirked. "I'm having as much luck understanding the text as you had when Lyrie and Lyle invented their own language."

"They still speak in that gibberish occasionally." Syra heaved a long-suffering sigh. "They do it just to vex me. I know it."

"Send them to me, I'll put them to work," I joked. "I think the soup's done."

Syra nudged me out of the way so she could stir the soup a few more times. When she was satisfied, she took it off the burner.

"I long for the day when I can get high-quality fruits again," she sighed. "It's too damn expensive. I have to either pick good food or electricity. Some months, I'm highly tempted to break out the candles."

"Things will get better soon," I assured her. "Provided another race of aliens hell-bent on screwing us over doesn't show up, of course."

"What are the odds of that?"

"Don't make me think about it," I joked. "I like to

think the rest of the universe understands that our poor planet needs a break."

"There's that relentless optimism." Sa'lok appeared beside me and pressed a kiss onto my cheek. "Can I help with anything?"

"Grab bowls from the cupboard," Syra directed. "Ladle the soup. Don't fill up the kid's bowls too much. Less in their bowls to start with means less on their shirts and my floors. Lyrie will fill up after two bites anyway, no matter how close to starvation she claims to be. Lyle will just eat the bread."

"Should I not fill a bowl for him?" Sa'lok asked.

"Please do," I said. "If he doesn't get a bowl, he'll feel terribly left out and remind us constantly of it for the rest of the night."

"Noted," Sa'lok chuckled. "Rearing human babies is a science, isn't it?"

"More like a war," Syra laughed. "I wouldn't trade it for anything, though."

"Ma," Lyrie bounded into the kitchen. "Can we eat outside tonight?"

"I'm not sure about that, hon," Syra said. Lyrie couldn't see from where she stood, but I saw the flash of nervousness in my sister's eyes. Sa'lok saw it, too.

"The planet's safer than it's been in a year," Sa'lok said. "I think we should take advantage."

"Besides," I chimed in, sidling up to Sa'lok. "We've got a professional planet protector to keep watch."

"Please, ma?" Lyrie begged, slipping her hand into Sa'lok's.

Syra smiled and sighed.

"I know when I'm outnumbered," she laughed. "All right. I need you and your brother to set the table, Lyrie."

"Okay," she nodded and bounded back out of the room.

"She's not coming back, is she?" I joked.

"Nope," Syra chuckled. "Sa'lok, fill their bowls, but leave them here. They need to get better about doing things on their own."

"You got it."

Sa'lok filled all of our bowls while Syra took her loaf out of the oven. My mouth watered at the sight of it.

"That smells amazing."

"I should hope so," Syra said. "I followed grandma's recipe down to the letter."

"Is that her rosemary butter bread?" I gawked.

"It sure is," Syra grinned.

"I haven't eaten that since before she passed."

"That's why I made it. You almost died too many times this month. We're celebrating your survival."

Out of habit, I tested my ribs. They were healing up

nicely but were still sore to the touch. Sa'lok, on the other hand, was completely healed.

I didn't hide my jealousy. I could be healed up, too, if I had teeny robots in my bones repairing me constantly.

We carried our plates and bowls outside to the backyard. Syra had a porch that looked out into the forest. The sun had set only moments ago. The sky was still orange and pink, but the bioluminescent plants of the forest had started glowing already.

"How pretty." Sa'lok and I shared a smile as we took our seats across from each other. Lyle wanted to sit beside me. Lyrie made it clear she wanted to sit next to Sa'lok. Syra took the head of the table.

"Ma, where's our food?" Lyle asked.

"Back in the kitchen," Syra said. "Did you expect me to serve you?"

Lyle knew a trick question when he heard one. Without another word, he and Lyrie went back inside to retrieve their dinner.

As Syra had predicted, the twins took no more than two bites, then insisted they were full. Sa'lok quickly finished his dinner so that he could play a round of tag with the kids.

"He's good with them," Syra commented as she helped herself to another slice of bread, thick with butter.

"He really is," I nodded. "I'll have to bring him

around more often."

"I don't think you'll have a choice. The kids have adopted him as one of their own. You'll be lucky if you're allowed to leave with him."

"Perhaps, we can stay the night?" I suggested. "If it's no trouble to you, of course."

"You're never a bother, sister." Syra squeezed my hand. "Not even when you're flying all over the planet, dancing with death."

"That's a highly poetic way of describing what I do," I chuckled.

"I'd rather say that to the neighbors than tell them you're a hellion who gets trapped under rocks far too often for someone who's supposed to be a pilot."

"Yeah, stick with the poetry," I laughed.

Something on the ground caught my eye. I glanced down at it. Growing between the cracks of the wood patio was a small, bright green vine. Thinking of the Puppet Master, and how he'd saved all of us, I reached down and gently stroked the little vine.

To my surprise, it wrapped its tendril around my finger.

Life hummed through the little plant like a tiny heartbeat.

The Puppet Master was still with us.

And life, here with my mate and my family, was good.

LETTER FROM ELIN

Thank you.

Thank you so much for coming with me on this crazy ride!

From the very first moment I had the image of Vrehx and Jeneva in the cave, to planning out the final battle, this has been a writing adventure unlike anything I'd ever attempted.

I've loved every minute of it - even when it was tough.

And you've been with me from the beginning, making all of this possible.

What's next?

I'm returning to the world of the Star Breed - if you haven't visited keep reading!

Given: Star Breed Book One

When a renegade thief and a genetically enhanced mercenary collide, space gets a whole lot hotter!

Thief Kara Shimsi has learned three lessons well - keep her head down, her fingers light, and her tithes to the syndicate paid on time.

But now a failed heist has earned her a death sentence - a one-way ticket to the toxic Waste outside the dome. Her only chance is a deal with the syndicate's most ruthless enforcer, a wolfish mountain of genetically-modified muscle named Davien.

The thought makes her body tingle with dread-or is it heat?

Mercenary Davien has one focus: do whatever is necessary to get the credits to get off this backwater mining colony and back into space. The last thing he wants is a smart-mouthed thief - even if she does have the clue he needs to hunt down whoever attacked the floating lab he and his created brothers called home.

Caring is a liability. Desire is a commodity. And love could get you killed.

Keep reading for a sneak peek!

XOXO,

Elin

PLEASE DON'T FORGET TO LEAVE A REVIEW!

Readers rely on your opinions, and your review can help others decide on what books they read. Make sure your opinion is heard and leave a review where you purchased this book!

Don't miss a new release! You can sign up for release alerts at both Amazon and Bookbub:

bookbub.com/authors/elin-wyn

amazon.com/author/elinwyn

For a free short story, opportunities for advance review copies, release news and the occasional cat picture, please join the newsletter!

https://elinwynbooks.com/newsletter-signup/

And don't forget the Facebook group, where I post sneak peeks of chapters and covers!

https://www.facebook.com/groups/ElinWyn/

GIVEN: SNEAK PEEK

K ARA

IT WAS all Juda's fault.

I kicked him out of my bed three weeks ago for cheating on me, but apparently, he wasn't done screwing me over.

I crouched low on the roof of the abandoned gambling den across the street from Sary's "general store" and cursed the limp-dicked bastard all over again.

There wasn't a lot of traffic at this time of day. Not that that meant much in Ghelfi; the thieves' city never truly slept. There was no point in waiting for night, like in the old vids Mom used to watch over and over. Like all sealed cities on the surface of Neurea, lighting in Ghelfi varied throughout the day's cycle, but never to a true night.

I saw real night, once. I stowed away on the back of a surface crawler that was heading to Lashell. I don't know why, somehow I'd thought it would be better if I got out of Ghelfi, started over somewhere else.

The velvet sky, studded with stars, shone clean and cold. Perfect. Not like the barely organized chaos of the cities.

But halfway there, the crawler broke down, had to be towed back. I realized then that there was no way out. Not for me.

In the old vids, everything always turned out alright, something swooped in at the last minute to save the day.

That's how you knew they were only lies.

So here I was, half-hidden among old wires and debris that had been kicked up to the top of the store years ago, long forgotten. Watching time slip away on the chrono, crossing my fingers to old gods I didn't believe in.

"What'cha doing?"

I jumped, furious with myself.

Bani crouched next to me. His dark brown hair

hung down in his face, but I could still see the twinkle in his eye. Snuck up on me and was proud of it, little bastard.

I socked him gently in the arm, just enough to let him know I cared.

"Everybody's looking for you, Kara," he said under his breath. He didn't look at me but instead kept his eyes scanning across the street, trying to see what I was interested in. Smart kid.

I ran my hand through my own tangle of hair. It was past time to cut it, but things had been a little busy lately.

"How mad is Xavis?" I really didn't want to know the answer.

Bani shrugged one bony shoulder. "He's playing it down a little bit, but I think he's pretty steamed. If you, of all people, don't show up by the end of the tithe, he's gonna lose a lot of face."

A light crackled, the burnt smell of frying wires wafted by. But I wasn't paying attention to the noise or to the stink of ozone that permeated the air of Ghelfi. If Xavis really was mad, I was in trouble.

I shoved the thought far to the back of my head. Nothing to do about it but keep moving.

A shuffling sound below surprised me, and I risked another glance over the ledge. A miner, wrapped in rags so filthy there was no telling the gender, half-staggered down the street. He, she, whatever, paused in front of Sary's storefront, then stumbled inside.

Ice gripped my spine. Rings willing, he'd be quick. Claim whatever he came to trade, and get out. Not stay there, spinning stories of life in the Waste, screwing my timetable.

"Is that the job?" Bani's wide eyes fixed me. "A snatch and grab on the miners after they bring in the dust?"

I rolled my eyes. "They're just trying to get by, same as us." Besides, credits were no good to me, not with so little time to clean them. But the antonium dust the miners brought in was untraceable. 'Dust knows no provenance' was the saying. I just needed to get enough of it.

Agonizing minutes passed until he left. I glanced at my chrono again. If she didn't show up today, I didn't have a backup plan. This was my backup plan. No more nets to catch my fall.

I closed my eyes to try to find the calm, cold center within that had kept me alive so far on the streets of Ghelfi, and waited. I didn't need to see, didn't need to check the time. I could only wait and listen.

Finally, the sound came. The sharp click of stiletto heels across the permasteel walkway. I opened my eyes and leaned forward ever so slightly to peer down the street.

There she was. Charro's secret indulgence. Silver hair teased into a high fall down her back, her face paint marked her as one of Sary's working girls. When I first found out about Charro's extracurricular activities, I'd half thought of sending a note to Sary, stir up the nest a bit. Then I started thinking long term. That'd been almost two years ago.

Two years of planning and waiting brought to a crash by that bastard Juda. I should have gutted him like a fish instead of just kicking him out.

Bani glanced at her and then looked up at me, frowning.

"That's your mark?" He risked another look but I pulled him back sharply by the collar of his jacket.

He glared at me, with all the scorn a preteen could manage. "I know her. She works the landing pad. Even if she did have the sort of money you're going to need to get out of trouble with Xavis, she isn't gonna be carrying it with her on a job." His eyes narrowed. "So what are you really up to?"

I grinned. I couldn't help it. I wasn't pleased to have to use this job to get out of the hole Juda left me in, but it was pretty brilliant.

"Just keep your eye on the alley, kid, okay?"

I checked my chrono again, but I didn't need to. I'd

timed this pattern so often. Like clockwork, the shadows of Charro's two goons came into focus on the tinted plex of the storefront. Just like every other time I'd watched, they paced back and forth, no doubt joking about their boss and his hobby.

"They're supposed to be guarding the back room, but he always kicks them out when she visits." I checked the time again, stupid habit. Couldn't help it. "He might be there, but he's more than a little distracted right now."

I worked my way across the roof, down to the collection of rubble in the back alley that had let me gain my vantage point.

Bani followed me and I glared at him.

"Stay up here," I snarled. "I don't know how this is going to turn out."

"Then you'll need a second pair of hands."

The kid had a point, but I'd be damned if I was going to let him have it.

"No, I need a second pair of eyes." His shoulders sagged a little. But I couldn't be sure he wouldn't follow me anyway.

"Besides, I don't know if I can trust you on this job." His white face told me my words hit their mark. Hated to do it, but I didn't want to be worried about him. I was in enough trouble as it was.

His face slid out of sight as I worked my way down the trash heap.

Even before I crossed the street, the bitter stench of the acid bombs I'd planted clawed at my throat. The air recirculators only worked intermittently in this neighborhood, and in the alley, the smell almost forced me to my knees.

That the miner walked by without flinching, I could understand. I'd heard too much time in an environmental suit would have you smelling nothing but rubber. But the silver-haired doxy must have been high on something to not notice something was wrong.

No time to linger in the alley. Microcams swept every ninety seconds, watching, waiting for anything out of the ordinary.

I dashed to the hiding space I'd carved out of the fallen wall that backed up to Sary's, and held my breath, trying to hear over the drumming of my heartbeat. The rushing in my ears slowed, and I poked my head out. Still all clear.

Nobody in their right mind would take on Sary, he ran half the games in town, and word in the pits said he wanted to take control of the city over from Xavis. Unlikely, but still, not someone I really wanted after me. But if the choice was Sary or Xavis himself....well, it was a sucky choice.

I counted, waiting for the next clear moment to

check on the results of the clustered acid bombs, then ran back around the corner.

Ninety seconds is a long time.

Ninety seconds is long enough to make one chip in the wall a day until a section can be lifted away and replaced seamlessly.

Ninety seconds is long enough to plant one small acid bomb at a time, then wait for a few days for the smell to dissipate, for the interior wall that led to the vault to weaken, bit by bit, day by day.

Ninety seconds is long enough to die in the Waste, outside of the protection of the domes.

And if I didn't get my tithe to Xavis by tonight, that's where I'd end up.

DAVIEN

REALLY, everything would be so much easier if I just snapped the fat fool's neck. Only the endless lessons in control back on the ship kept my hands still at my sides, fingers barely flexing. The tips of my claws ran across my palms, bringing me back to focus.

"Davien, are you even listening to me?" Xavis rumbled.

And he wasn't a fool, even if I despised him. Xavis

had clawed his way to the top of the dirtiest pile to run Ghelfi. The trip to the top had been over the broken bodies of plenty of enemies. He'd stayed on his perch for over twenty Imperial years. I didn't have to do much research to know his methods hadn't changed.

Prime example: he'd hired me.

I focused on Xavis, only too aware I'd started to slip away into the hunt. Every moment here, stuck on this rock, was a delay I couldn't afford. Xavis, bastard though he might be, was my fastest way out of here. Well, the fastest way without an unacceptably high casualty count.

Xavis lounged in his hover chair, fingers tapping in annoyance well away from the control pad. The chair was as much affectation as convenience - he could walk just fine. Just liked to be able to loom over people.

"She's late," he growled. "She's never late."

I didn't need to ask who he meant. He'd been on a tear about his precious Kara for hours, first calling her his brightest find, then cursing her ingratitude.

The large room I'd come to think of as the receiving hall was mostly empty now, just the regular workers at their terminals around the edges, cleaning credits, shifting funds until they could be transferred into the most secure banks in the Empire. Repetitive, mind-numbing, but crucial to any modern criminal enterprise. The low drone as they worked filled the otherwise quiet room.

The last traces of the dark festivities of the last day had almost been erased. All day and night long, denizens of Ghelfi's underworld had streamed in, bringing their tribute to the acknowledged boss of the city, doing their best, or worst, to please a capricious overlord. The whole affair had been boring, and stupidly inefficient.

But the archaic ritual soothed his ego and had been an opening to a job. At the last tithing, some idiot with more guts than brains had tried to take Xavis out. He'd failed to account for the force shield over the hover chair, but his explosives did thin out Xavis' bodyguards considerably.

Bad luck for them, perfect timing for me. When Doc had commanded we all enter the escape pods, she'd made it clear we were to jump as randomly as possible. It should have worked, should have drawn the attackers away from the *Daedalus*, but it had been six standard weeks since I'd crashed here, and I hadn't had a signal from her or any of my brothers.

If I was on my own, I needed credits. And I needed a lot of them.

Six weeks had been enough to battle my way up the ranks of Xavis' enforcers. Not that they were slouches, but they didn't have my, shall we say, advantages.

A commotion at the entrance to the room drew my attention, and I angled for a better position at the front of Xavis's chair. The dais we stood on served as an excellent vantage point for the room, allowing me to take in any suspicious movements at a glance. I'd argued to get rid of the scarlet drapery behind us, observing it provided too obvious of a hiding place. He'd refused. Like the dais, it was all about show.

The scuffle at the doorway turned out to be two enforcers dragging a third man between them. Beneath the new scrapes and swelling around his eye, I recognized him. Marcus, Martin, something like that. A low-level hustler who worked the dive bars near the station. Rigged games of chance, targeting travelers who wouldn't be around long enough to make a fuss.

Xavis waved me back into place, and I relaxed, just a tad. This wasn't a threat to his authority, just another loser trapped here.

The enforcers tossed the poor sap onto the lowest level of the dais and stepped back, waiting for orders.

"Malik," Xavis coaxed the hover chair to the edge of the dais, watching the human wreck below take shuddering breaths. "You didn't appear for the tithing last night." He floated down, a pale mass of malevolence, eyes narrowed.

I stepped behind him. I didn't expect trouble from

Malik, but there'd be hell to pay if I wasn't where Xavis expected me, especially when he was in this mood.

"Well?" Xavis's low voice was almost pleasant, but a thread of malice wound through it, unmistakable. "We've known each other for so long, I'm surprised that you've disappointed me."

"I'm sorry, Lord Xavis," the man mumbled. Probably had lost a few teeth. "My youngest has been down with the Batdu pox, the medicine was so much..." He gulped. "I thought I could make it up before the tithing."

"Oh?" Xavis's eyes glittered. "How is the poor thing doing now?"

"Better now, Lord Xavis. Thank you."

"You should have told me, I would have lent you the money."

Sure he would have. At rates that would mean he'd own the service of the entire family.

"But, as it is, we have a problem that needs to be sorted out." Xavis made a show of tapping his fingers, as if considering, but that sharp brain had already decided on the punishment, I was sure. This was just to terrorize the hustler, and send a message to everyone else in the room.

"I'd forgotten about your lovely family," he purred. "The oldest is twelve now, as I recall?"

The man shifted uneasily. "Yes, my lord. But she's not very strong..."

"I'm sure a more active life will be good for her. She'll have her own tithe to pay, starting next cycle."

"What?" The man pushed himself to his feet, protesting.

Idiot.

Xavis flicked a finger, and I sprang to the front of the chair to grab the beaten hustler by the front of his jacket. I lifted him off the floor and shook him until his head snapped back.

He pushed feebly against my grip.

"I wouldn't try it," I growled, and he froze.

I'm not sure what it is about my voice. On the ship, with my brothers, no one had a problem with it. In all the training vids we watched, I never thought I sounded that different. But here, on this worthless rock at the fringe of the Empire, all I had to do was speak, and the humans cowered.

Weak.

Prey.

I snarled, and the acrid scent of urine assaulted me. The fucker had wet himself. Apparently, he hadn't liked the points of my teeth, either.

"I suggest you comply, little man. What choice do you have?"

He stared at me, face pale beneath the marks of the beating, but finally nodded. It wasn't much of a motivational speech, but it was the truth. No one on Neurea had a lot of choices.

"I think you can release him now, Davien." The smug tone of Xavis's voice told me he'd gotten what he wanted. He hadn't had to send a usually reliable worker to the Wastes, and he'd picked up extra leverage at the same time.

I lowered the man back to his feet. His legs buckled, but he scrambled away from me on hands and knees. Idiot. I wasn't the worst monster in the room.

The rest of the negotiations were predictably short and one-sided. The hustler left, and the business in the room resumed its quiet drone.

"I've decided." Xavis's voice cracked like a whip as he floated back to the top of the dais. "An example must be made."

I waited below for orders.

"Find Kara Shimshi. Bring her to me."

Despite my better instincts, I grinned.

The hunt was on.

KARA

. . .

I WAITED, checking my chrono obsessively, preparing the last items, until the first moment the microcams flew away. The way was clear, but not for long.

Ninety.

The false covering of the weakened wall came off easily. I set it on the ground next to me, hands shaking.

Any loud, unexpected sound in the area would summon the microcams out of their regular routine, and my ninety seconds would be over fast.

Ideally, I would have waited days after the last of my corrosive little beasties had done their work. That would have been plenty of time for the area to be safe. But now I'd have to work the job despite a dulled sense of touch through an acid-proof glove.

One tentative push through the jagged opening, another against the half-dissolved back wall of the safe.

Eighty.

A final push, and nothing but empty space beyond. I was in.

The opening was narrow, barely wide enough to slide my hand through, but there was no time to widen it. Now that I'd breached their security, there'd never be an opening like this again.

Even through the glove, I could feel the triangular prism shape of the antonium vials. I grabbed one and, slower than I would've liked, eased it out to place in the pouch I'd unfolded while waiting.

Each vial would nestle in a separate pocket. Antonium had a reputation for nasty surprises when jostled about.

Sweat ran down my back, measuring the seconds in fear. I'd wipe it off later. No time now.

Eyes watering from the fumes that still lingered in the alleyway, I reached through the gap for another vial, then another.

Seventy.

The urge to just grab a handful, stuff them in my pack and be gone shook my chest. But the hole wasn't large enough for a fisted hand. I had to wrap my fingers underneath each prism and slowly coax it out towards me.

Another one nestled in its pocket.

The sting of the acid against the flesh of my arm began to burn. I hadn't thought it would still be so potent when I came in for the job, I'd assumed the gloves would be enough. I reached for another vial. Better some scars on my arm than to be tossed into the Waste.

Fifty.

"My hands are smaller, let me do it."

Crap. "What are you doing here?" I hissed between my teeth, trying not to split my attention, and knowing I was failing.

"I want to help," Bani whispered back. "Here, I

can..." As he reached towards the opening, his foot caught the edge of the section of wall I'd removed.

The sheet of permasteel wobbled once, twice, and then fell with a clatter that could be heard for blocks. The shrill whir of the microcams changing direction, picking up speed, told me in no uncertain terms we'd been noticed.

I snatched my hand back from the opening. One last vial, no time to gently pack it. The long strap of the bag went over my head, and I grabbed Bani.

"I'm sorry..." he started.

"Just run," was all I had time to say.

"You there, wait!" The heavy footfalls of the goons as they emerged from the shop punctuated the sound of the microcams.

The chase was on.

I grinned. I couldn't help it. I'd been running through the streets and alleys of Ghelfi for over half my life. The hit of adrenaline, the intense focus on the next step, the next jump, left no room for any other worries.

In the alley behind the row of gambling dens that all paid tithe to Xavis, we could hear the murmur of winners and losers, a soft rush of voices that faded as we darted down another small passageway, twisting and turning. But still, the cams were on us. The goons didn't need to be fast, just keep their tracking on.

The smell of fried noodles hit me; we were behind

Artin's place. He'd always looked the other way when I snagged leftover food from the trash as a kid. My stomach growled, heedless of the current crisis.

If we got out of this, if I survived the tithe, I'd treat Bani to a feast.

If.

Into the oldest section of Ghelfi city, alleys filled with broken parts not even worth the recycle bounty, snarled nests of wires cracking between buildings, dodging the dangling streamers, because you never knew what was still live and what could kill you.

"Kara," Bani gasped from behind me. "I can't keep up." His voice broke, sobbing for air as we ran.

"Just a bit farther, I promise." I hated promising. I hate lying and promises too often end up that way, at least in our world. But if we could just make it a few blocks further, we had a chance.

Legs aching, we sprinted across the street of the main bazaar, dodging the tramline filled with tourists and miners and gamblers and suckers that all thought that here, on the fringe of the Empire, they'd make their dreams come true.

"Through here," I called over my shoulder, and darted between two dingy storefronts, back in the shelter of the alleys.

On the streets, it was too easy for a goon or a drone to take a shot. Needlers were illegal in the Empire, which meant everyone seemed to have at least a pair on Neurea as a badge of citizenship. Everyone except me. Needlers, pretty much all guns, made me queasy. Not for the first time, I wondered if I should re-evaluate that plan.

The back ways, left over from when the huge assembler machines had formed the basic structures of the city back in the day, zigged and zagged in a tangled pattern. Their creators probably thought it made perfect sense, but they were all long dead.

Finally, the maintenance shaft I'd been homing in on came within sight. My fingers laced in the grill, jerking it off as I skidded to a stop.

"Told you..." I was talking to the air. Bani was gone.

Rings. I needed to get away, get clear of the area and to Xavis and get shit straightened out. It wasn't my fault the stupid kid tagged along. Hell, it was his fault we were running now.

Damn it.

I stashed the bag in the shaft. No point risking it, even if I was an idiot.

I headed back the way we'd come, slower this time. If Bani had just gotten lost, that would be one thing... but if he'd been caught, I didn't feel like rushing my head into a noose.

"Get your hands off me, you jerk!" The yelling made a great beacon and a warning. I poked my head around the corner and pulled back right away. They'd caught him, the darker haired of the goons holding Bani's thin frame pressed against the wall of the old water plant, seepage running out from under the wall, turning the dust underfoot to mud.

The kid kicked in his grip, but he'd need to weigh at least four times as much to make any difference. I risked another look, discarding options as fast as I came up with them. A crackle overhead caught my attention. Maybe....

Digging through the rubbish, I found a length of scrap wire. I pulled out my knife and started wrapping it.

It wasn't a great plan, but it was all I had. I eased out from the corner and waved. Bani saw me, and I pointed overhead, then to the ledge of a boarded up window next to him. His eyes widened, but he nodded.

Then he bit the hell out of the arm of the goon holding him.

Bastard hadn't expected that, and he dropped Bani. Instead of falling like a rock, Bani wiggled, twisting his body so he caught the edge of the windowsill with the tips of his fingers.

"Don't fall, kid," I muttered, and threw my knife into the tangle of wires overhead.

For a long moment, it looked like my gamble had

failed. The knife tangled in the cluster above, the long wire I'd wrapped around the blade trailing into the damp dirt below. But nothing was happening. Then, with a shriek of metal on metal, the whole tangled mess tumbled down, catching the goons and the bots in their net.

Both thugs lay in the damp ground, twitching slightly. It didn't look like the shock had been enough to kill them, even if the electronics were fried. One small knot untangled in my gut. I'd made it so far without killing anyone, at least that I knew about.

Movement on the wall caught my attention. Bani still clung there, pressed tight against the wall. I guess, if that was my choice today, I could live with it.

Bani worked his way hand over hand down the windowsill towards me and dropped to the ground, well clear of the danger zone. He looked up at me, grinning. "That was great."

I ran my hand through my hair and smothered the urge to shake him. "Belay that. The cams probably got our faces, probably sent them to the servers. The trouble isn't over."

My hand drifted to my side, fingers ghosting over the sheath. "And I've lost my favorite knife."

His face fell. "Thanks for coming back for me," he whispered.

I punched his arm. "Of course, idiot." Maybe I

should have hugged him. But that would have been weird for both of us.

He must have known what I meant, because he perked right back up, nearly skipping in circles around me as we headed back to the hiding place. "Did you get enough to make tithe? Maybe extra to sweeten Xavis back up? He's only angry because he likes you, you know."

At his age, the tithe would be pretty minimal. It was for most kids, made it easy to agree, trade a little of the take for protection, for food. For the semblance of a family, when you had no one else.

Xavis had always pushed me harder, said I had a talent for the game that would be a shame not to develop. Unfortunately, his idea of encouragement was to push, and push hard.

My tithes had always been twice the other kids' in our band of castaways and orphans.

But still, it was better than starving.

I'd pulled eight vials out from the safe before Bani had shown up to 'help.' "It'll be enough, maybe even a little left over as a buffer." For all the chaos, even with having to push the timeline on the plan, it had worked. Xavis would forgive me being late with such a haul. The vise around my chest finally started to loosen. It was gonna be alright.

"After I check in, let's go hit up old Artin's place, get some station-style noodles?"

Bani nodded and started chattering about all the other fabulous treats in the street stands on the way. I half listened to him, half paid attention to the noise of the bazaar, the smells and sounds from all over the System. Things were going to work out. I could find a new long-term job, something that would really...

We turned the final corner back to the maintenance shaft and froze. Shock flipped a switch, filling my veins with fire.

"Hey!" I shouted. "Get away from that!"

A black-uniformed man hunched over my hiding place. The grill had been tossed into the alley and he crouched, head bowed down, peering into the shaft. He didn't flinch. I reached for my knife and swore at the empty sheath.

Instead, I grabbed a cracked tile, discarded years ago, and flung it at the guy. A rushing noise filled my ears, drowning out the city, Bani, everything. I'd gone through way too much hassle to lose the haul to a scavenger like that.

Except this wasn't like any scavenger I'd ever seen. Too neat, too clean. I would have thought he was military, if the Empire ever bothered to send anyone this far out.

The invader might have ignored my shouts, but the

edge of the tile cracked against his shoulder. There was something wrong with his movements as the black form slowly rose and turned my way.

His face was covered by a dark helmet, but all my attention was focused on the satchel in his hand. My satchel. My vials. My only hope.

"Get away!" I shrieked and tore towards him. I might not have my knife, but you didn't survive in Ghelfi City without learning a few things about a street fight. He might have been bigger than me, but I could count on desperation to lend me extra strength.

This day just wasn't going to stop, was it? I had to have that satchel. I flung myself at the dark shape, snatching the loop of the bag as I went by.

My own momentum snapped me back. The black-uniformed presence didn't move, didn't speak. I rushed at him, hoping to knock him over, get him to loosen his grip on my satchel.

Nothing. He stood as immovable as the rocks outside in the Waste. I grabbed another tile, ignoring the sting of the sharp edge that cut my hands, and smashed my fist with its improvised blade against the black helmet.

Didn't even scratch it. What the hell was this thing? I made another snatch at the satchel, pulling until the muscles in my arms screamed.

Suddenly, the motionless figure snapped. He

twisted, shaking me like a toy at the end of the string, until one final flip sent me flying into the opposite wall. Someone dropped a pile of permasteel bricks on my head, and blackness took me.

CLICK HERE to get Given now!

https://elinwynbooks.com/star-breed/

ABOUT THE AUTHOR

I love old movies – *To Catch a Thief, Notorious, All About Eve* — and anything with Katherine Hepburn in it. Clever, elegant people doing clever, elegant things.

I'm a hopeless romantic.

And I love science fiction and the promise of space.

So it makes perfect sense to me to try to merge all of those loves into a new science fiction world, where dashing heroes and lovely ladies have adventures, get into trouble, and find their true love in the stars!